THE TWELFTH ROOM

GUERNICA WORLD EDITIONS 86

Quest'opera è stata tradotta
con il contributo del Centro per il libro
e la lettura del Ministero della Cultura italiano

This work has been translated
with the contribution of the Centre for
Books and Reading of the Italian Ministry of Culture

CENTRO
PER IL LIBRO
E LA LETTURA

THE TWELFTH ROOM

Teresa Antonacci

Translated from Italian by

Connie Guzzo-McParland

GUERNICA
World
EDITIONS

TORONTO–CHICAGO–BUFFALO–LANCASTER (U.K.)
2023

Guernica Editions Founder: Antonio D'Alfonso

Michael Mirolla, editor
Cover and design: Allen Jomoc Jr.
Interior design: Jill Ronsley, suneditwrite.com

Guernica Editions Inc.
287 Templemead Drive, Hamilton (ON), Canada L8W 2W4
2250 Military Road, Tonawanda, N.Y. 14150-6000 U.S.A.
www.guernicaeditions.com

Distributors:
Independent Publishers Group (IPG)
600 North Pulaski Road, Chicago IL 60624
University of Toronto Press Distribution (UTP)
5201 Dufferin Street, Toronto (ON), Canada M3H 5T8

First edition.
Printed in Canada.

Legal Deposit—Third Quarter
Library of Congress Catalog Card Number: 2023935218
Library and Archives Canada Cataloguing in Publication
Title: The twelfth room / Teresa Antonacci ; translated from
Italian by Connie Guzzo-McParland.
Other titles: Dodicesima stanza. English
Names: Antonacci, Teresa, author. | Guzzo-McParland, Connie,
1947- translator.
Series: Guernica world editions (Series) ; 86.
Description: Series statement: Guernica world editions ; 86 |
Translation of: La dodicesima stanza.
Identifiers: Canadiana (print) 20230216285 | Canadiana (ebook)
20230216382 | ISBN 9781771839259 (softcover) | ISBN
9781771839266 (EPUB)
Classification: LCC PQ4901.N76 D63 2023 | DDC 853/.92—dc23

I.

IF I HAD BEEN BORN a boy, I would have been an engineer, like my father. I would have played soccer with him, trying my best not to disappoint him; maybe I would have gone bicycling with him, or gone fishing on the terraces of Polignano, if not, on a boat or to Cala Incina. In short, I would have done "normal" things, as befits a male from a good family. I would have made him a grandfather, handing down his name and surname, with the same initials embroidered on shirts and handkerchiefs; because, if I had been born a boy, surely, I would have been named Francesco, after my father's father. They had not "crippled" his name, as they do for female names: grandfather Francesco had not become grandfather Ciccio, and grandfather Giuseppe remained so, just like my father Giacomo. Do you not see how childbirth, a female act par excellence, the first causal effect of generational transmission, does not have the same mnemonic value as a name? Well ... everyone was expecting a boy, but I was born. Already, squabbling and acts of spitefulness had begun within the family because of the name. Mom had been adamant about it: her mother-in-law's name was unpronounceable.

"Finella … is one of those names that would make one give birth to an already complexed daughter!" she told her husband. "I'll never call her that!" Until then, perhaps that had been the first truly autonomous decision in her entire life. Even her mother, after all, whom they called Nenetta in place of Antonia, didn't have much of a name. "But still better than Finella!" she had commented sarcastically to her husband, who had taken the matter head-on as if it were a personal affront. And maybe it was. So, after examining the names of aunts, cousins, wedding witnesses and more or less nice friends, in the end, Alina had won. In homage to the song *Pasqualino Maraja* and its author Domenico Modugno, our illustrious fellow *paesano* and my father's school friend.

From grandmother Nenetta I had inherited green eyes and red hair and the twelve-room house in the historic center of Polignano—the house where the grandparents had gone to live when just married, and which had been willed to me when I turned eighteen. Fortunately, I hadn't inherited my grandmother's "onions." When I saw them, I asked Grandpa Giuseppe why they called her bunions "onions" when, unlike onions, they didn't have the slightest roundness, with those pointed lumps and those nails as sharp as hooks. He, who was the only one who always explained things without mincing words, simply replied: "Onions on your feet hurt so much at times that they make you cry like the onions you eat when you clean them!" I had looked at him skeptically but had no reason to doubt his words. It immediately seemed an injustice, especially if I considered that it was those same "weeping onions" that prevented grandmother Nenetta from running left and right around Polignano with me. From then on, I associated onions both with unhappiness and with the satisfaction that the unhappiness engendered: given grandmother's diminishing company, I was able to take advantage exclusively of grandfather Giuseppe, his perfect feet and his stories.

Unforgettable were the moments spent with him wandering through the alleys, nose up in the air, looking for physical evidence of his stories on the older buildings, discovering traces of the history of lived lives: the seat carved in the walls, with the chains to pillory the evildoers. "They chained them without trousers or underpants, to make them feel more ashamed!" he said. And the bust of Queen Giovanna and King Luigi, up there, on the second row of windows of the candid white palace that had housed them, when they reigned over Polignano. Rusty scissors hung outside the windows, with their jaws open "against the evil eye," and the dried garlic necklaces to decorate the jambs and railings of stairs and under the arches. "To drive away evil spirits," *cattoive* in Polignanese dialect for evil. Every single glimpse of Polignano, every hidden or unknown corner reminded me of grandfather Giuseppe and my imperfect childhood. Perfection is not for everyone.

My father and my mother had been engaged since *liceo,* senior high school. Their families had strongly sought the union more for economic interest than for anything else, but it seems that this is how things were done then. Grandfather Giuseppe was an entrepreneur in the oil sector; grandfather Francesco grew almonds: they had united lands and children, monopolizing the Polignano economy and climbing the social ladder with increased prestige. They had planned their children's whole lives, not just engagement and marriage but also university and career paths. In short, my parents were the classic middle-class spoiled children, in a period, the postwar one, strongly marked by all kinds of rebirths.

They hadn't had a hard time fitting in the world of work, as graduates, not that they needed it, it must be said, but their being "professionals" added further points to the prestige of families. After the wedding party, the sumptuousness of which was essential—otherwise who knows what they would have thought in the town—they had gone to live in the house that mom had brought as a dowry and dad had furnished because it was customary for the female to bring the house and the male the furnishings. They had started waiting for me and had done so for over ten years. Years of waiting, delays, false hopes and disappointments. And a lot of money spent on gynecological examinations, because the blame was always to be attributed to the female genital system and never to the male one. Each time grandmother Nenetta, to console mother, said to her: «*dà na atte delusiaune atten a léziaune; iavvedai ca aqquann main tu aspitt, ialavai na soppraise*», a Polognese proverb that means, "You must learn a lesson from a bad disappointment; when you least expect it, however, you will receive surprises."

When they were already resigned to childlessness, I arrived. It happened when my mother was teaching Latin and Greek in a *liceo classico,* classical high school, in Bari: obviously, she was put immediately to rest, served and revered by the two grandmothers who had demanded that she stay at home, to avoid any danger of losing that child, as precious as it was unexpected. My father, on the other hand, had gone into hiding: too many women in the house, all unbearable! He was an engineer and worked in the Railways: he had entered it when they were still called *Ferrovie dello Stato,* the State Railways, and then he had adapted to the various corporate restyling that had followed over the years.

"They are controversial years," he repeated in perfect Italian, being careful not to reveal the dialectal cadence, even when he was at home those rare times he spoke. He repeated continuously that they had worked miracles in those years, and that the Railways had to thank him and those like him, who were planning new plants and traction electronic vehicles, which would have been our future. He had no other topics to talk about. He was always travelling around Italy to clean up messes, experiment with new ways or create infrastructures from scratch, ready to stop construction sites for orders received from his higher-ups, if not from the judiciary.

My parents had started getting mutually impatient when they found out they were expecting a child, in an

absolutely anachronistic temporality: normal couples
would have been at the peak of happiness, especially
old-fashioned ones like them. They, on the other hand,
were in perennial disagreement about me, who was not
yet born. He dreamed of a male to take to construction sites and on train locomotives; she a little girl to
dress up like a doll and coddle in moments of emotional emptiness that the discontinued presence of her
husband arose. Emotional emptiness that was there
anyway, even when he was physically present. They
had started arguing precisely about this story as if their
quarrels could somehow invalidate the genetic laws
and impose one sex rather than the other. I was already
there to hear them: separated from them only by the
few layers of muscle and skin that enveloped the amniotic sac. Their shrill voices boomed in the void within,
violating my aqueous refuge. They disturbed me.

I was born at the stroke of the new year, completing the family picture only to upset it definitively. They
had even made a fuss about that, as if mom had done it
on purpose to go into labour on the last day of the year,
to bother everyone!

My childhood is locked in the heart, watertight,
emotionally circumscribable but with very little physical evidence of it. What remains is only a small group
of photos, those that I had liked most and that I was
able to hide in the bottom of the backpack that I had
brought with me the time that mom and I had sneaked
away like thieves from Polignano. Those few photos
were surprise shots, almost all stolen by grandfather
Giuseppe during our after-school or Sunday morning

jaunts. He said that for capturing the right photo moment one had to be well equipped, so he went out of the house with his shoulder bag, always too paunchy because of the camera. It was a Canon Pellix, I still remember it, with so many features that even he didn't know how to use: often he did not even notice that the roll of film was finished, so he kept on taking pictures that he never found again when he went to collect the prints from the photographer. In spite of everything, he had managed to immortalize me with the neat white lace dresses that were never white; with mother-of-pearl buttons dangling, when they were still there; with shoes in hand, those with the "eyes" that were so fashionable then, and I, barefoot, exploring pavements or meadows, roads or rocks. With my beloved books, which were often bigger than me, all intent on looking at the pictures or interpreting the captions in my own way which I was already able to read at the age of two.

"But was she born like this, already learned?" everyone asked, in that strange Italianized dialect that fully conveyed the idea and that almost never presupposed a benevolent comment: everyone felt obliged to comment on my character or my attitudes, my oddities which, according to them, were nothing more than the whims of a spoiled child.

"Another child would be needed!" they passed sentence. They were all good at talking when it involved criticizing. Grandfather Giuseppe was always saddened by these talks: he cut them short and quickly invented a mandatory commission on behalf of grandmother Nenetta. Sometimes he pretended to sneeze so he could take the handkerchief out of his pocket and wipe his eyes as if I didn't understand that his were tears and nothing else: when I pointed this out to him, he always denied it, because "boys never cry!" But it had happened to him many times.

I guess it was a sight to look at me while I was reading *I Promessi Sposi* or the *Divine Comedy*, if not Cicero, Ovid, Virgil or Aesop and his tales in the mother tongue. How I did it, I don't know. At first, it was a source of pride for Mom: she took me to class with her to show me off in front of her better pupils, little did it matter that they were fifteen years older than me. While she was having fun, proudly telling me that she had transmitted that genius passion for literature and archaic languages in my DNA, it was a burden for me to have to read on command for that wide-eyed audience that, at the end of the reading, attacked me with kisses and caresses, as if I were a freak. They could not conceive that books were my whole world: I, closed in the mirror of their pages, flew in Pindaric mode, mowed green meadows, milked cows and fed lambs, cultivated multi-coloured and multiform flowers with butterflies fluttering, and imagined from their colours the scent of ginger, cinnamon and cotton candy. Only books accepted me as I was, without ifs, ands, or buts, without reproach and punishment which, even if mild, deeply undermined my self-esteem.

Then the irreparable happened. It was a Saturday. I remember it well because I was watching television and Raffaella Carrà was there: she was the only one, in addition to the books and grandfather Giuseppe's speeches, who attracted my attention, with her frenetic way of shaking the blonde hair that I liked so much to imitate. My parents were fighting, as usual over me.

Dad just couldn't stand me.

"She's weird, too weird! And you and your father … you give in to her all the time!" he was saying to mom while I, interrupted in my imitation, had started wandering around the house barefoot, on tiptoe, to vent my nervousness. I think he was also telling me to stay still, but I didn't listen to him: he was just a distant echo that hummed in my ears. He looked at me with the same disgusted face as when mom cooked something he didn't like. His anger mounted. "It's a disgrace, this brat's rudeness!"

It was then that he finally said it: I was not the child he would have wanted. He repeated it over and over, perhaps to make sure I was listening, his unpleasant voice covering that of Raffaella's. I still remember the refrain of the song she sang, every now and then it whirls through my head. I intruded on their voices, shouting louder than them. When they quietened down, with all the seraphic calm that I had managed to recover, I said that it was seven hundred and fifty-eight days, fifteen hours, twenty minutes and two seconds that I had to put up with them and that I was tired. He looked at me in horror for a stingy handful of seconds, then he left the house slamming the door. Mom continued to stare at me petrified, with a look I had never seen before, then she took a pen and paper.

"Repeat what you said, love … how long have you been tolerating us?" she asked me. I replied by adding seven minutes and forty-eight seconds, as many as had passed since I had silenced them. She went to the calculator on the desk, the one with which they counted expenses and bills to pay; she hit on the keys, marking her results on a sheet of paper as the roll of paper spit them out. She remained there, resting on her chair, dishevelled like the rag doll that grandmother Nenetta had given me, with her arms at her sides and her eyes down. And I finally resumed my joyous fluttering around the house, with the little Raffaella song in my head that I had liked so much.

The next day, while Dad was at work, Mom took me to a doctor friend in his private practice. "I'm not taking her to an asylum," I had heard her say on the phone when she called him for an appointment, pretending to be calm, but wearing the same watery look I saw on her every time she quarrelled with Dad. A transparent liquidity made up of tears and doubts. Grandmother Nenetta, who was next to her, had begun to cry inconsolably as if someone dear to her had died. After the visit, the aquosity in Mom's eyes had increased considerably, but I hadn't noticed that much: I was all absorbed in remembering the single words that had been uttered by that strange doctor who hadn't even bothered to let me out of the room as they talked about me. As if I weren't there with them. As if I were deaf or blind, if not stupid!

In hindsight, I wondered if Mom was really worried about what the doctor told her or if she was just scared of talking about it with her husband and my grandparents.

"She is definitely schizophrenic," he told her. "Without a shadow of a doubt!" She had widened her eyes and had not spoken anymore, but she had not resigned herself to that diagnosis and she never stopped in her search for someone who could give a more plausible explanation for my absolutely incomprehensible behaviour. But those were dark years, in which everything that was outside of rational boxes was catalogued as schizophrenia, without any possibility of appeal.

Of course, when you know the truth, you can understand the whys of so many things, you can connect all the oddities and irrational behaviour or the small and large more or less expressed delusions, and above all, you can find so much familiarity in attitudes. In hindsight, I realized that I was the same as my father, with his mania for trains, his monothematic speeches, his standoffish character and his lack of emotional responses.

I asked Mom to explain the single words that connoted that "disorder" they said I was suffering from: she, who always spoke to me as if I were already grown up, at that grave moment picked me up and cuddled me.

"You know, there are things that cannot be explained to two-year-old girls," she told me. "I like you like this; you are my puppy and you always will be."

She had moved away from me and I was no longer able to see myself in her eyes. They looked like two puddles of dirty water, the kind you avoid when you come across them because you risk getting drenched with the first car that glides into it. I felt her cold and distant even when she was next to me. I reacted absurdly, provoking her and opposing any request from her, which never had a positive response from me. I did not understand that only in that manner could she be able to look at me more objectively. She "studied" me, in short. She even bought herself a notebook with a hard cover and that elastic band that I enjoyed pulling and extending so much, just to hear the dull snap it made on the cardboard: she wrote on it every day, noting down all the strange things she saw me do, and every evening she reread what she herself had written.

When I turned three, she enrolled me in the nursery school in Polignano, but she was systematically called to pick me up before she even arrived at her school in Bari. I screamed like a mad woman, apparently for no reason, and I was a nuisance to everyone. They were difficult moments, after which even grandfather Giuseppe could not calm me down.

"Separation anxiety!" said the psychologist every time she was called by the school director when I started to freak out. She always treated me smugly, never thoroughly investigating my strange reactions. She never thought of asking me directly what was happening in those moments. I would even have answered her, I wasn't stupid, as everyone told me instead. I was bothered by every slight variation in the routine, whether it was a "new" child sitting next to me or the snack served ten minutes later than expected; for me, everything had to remain stationary, unchanged: same games, same hours, same friends, and I even complained about cups and plates. I didn't even like that "feeling"—the need for everything to remain unchanged, but it happened and I couldn't do anything about it. And when it happened, I felt such uncontrollable anger build up inside that I would have smashed everything without even noticing.

Yes, if someone had asked me, I would have answered as well. But they never asked me anything. I remained the schizophrenic child, that fool. That crazy one to avoid absolutely.

II.

I HAD TO LIVE SOMEWHERE. THEREFORE, by force of circumstances, I grew up in the school in Bari where my mother taught. I knew the classrooms of that school inside out, with the walls peeling from the damage of restless students like me; with the library full of dust and casually abandoned tomes, yet to be catalogued. I listened to Latin and Greek sitting on the floor, in the belly of desks heavy with dust, violated by the scrapings of pens; I conversed with the spiders, hidden with their webs among the books; with the industrious ants always looking for crumbs on the floor, in the staff room; with butterflies, lightly amusing themselves among the branches of fleeting flowers that sprouted between one brick and another on the sidewalk of the outdoor gym. I gave everyone a name, flowers and animals. I knew them one by one. I made long speeches to them. They were the ones who convinced me not to speak out loud when we were together: I followed their advice because they would never deceive or judge me, while the rest of the world would. I closed myself in my universe made of numbers that crowded the thoughts or ritual refrains, and before returning to reality, I stopped in front of the closed door to wait for noises, feel scents, and observe materials. Before opening the handle on that door, I looked at it carefully: I checked if it was made of plastic, iron or brass, if the key was in the slot on the other side, or if it was lost, forgotten somewhere. Before opening that handle, I already imagined the walls or floors behind the door and when, decided, I finally opened it, it was only to take a step forward and then go back, go down three steps and stop again. Sitting in front of the spectacle of a variable disconnected from its context.

Obviously, with these assumptions, even the first grade had started badly. Grandfather Giuseppe often said: *"m (e) pèr (e) ca tengh na' figghi (e) cattoive!"*—"it seems I have a bad daughter". Given my father's lack of interest in my mother.

I don't remember ever being accompanied by my father to school. It was always my grandfather who did it. Every day he left me at the classroom door. Then he would loiter outside, in the courtyard in front, sitting at the bench waiting for the janitors to come out to call him so that he could take me back. It always happened. I annoyed everyone, both teachers and children; I constantly intervened interrupting the lesson, already knowing what the teacher was explaining. Often, I waited for her at the gate with apparently silly or all too specific questions, to which she did not even know what to answer. Nobody could stand me, often not even my mother.

Only grandfather Giuseppe was used to my rainbows, the explosion of colours and emotions that caused

my mood swings. He calmly took me back home to
grandmother Nenetta, since my mother would arrive
later. He calmed me down, entertaining me with the
tales of when he was a child; with war stories, which he
had unfortunately known, with his hardship and the
desire to return home to marry his Nenetta. He told
me about his mother, who was born very small and
they were afraid that she would die; of the difficulties,
diseases and famine they had had to endure immediately after the war; sometimes they even went hungry,
but then luckily, they managed to get through it all. He
often took me to the cemetery and along the tree-lined
avenues, strewn with pine needles and withered flowers; he told me of those faded faces on the tombstones,
of their stories, of what they had been or would have
become if they weren't dead; little girls' faces drowned
in the hatred of people or in the misfortune of disease,
sailors who died at sea, soldiers who left with him and
never returned, in whose graves there was nothing but
a medal or identification plate; our relatives, grandparents of the grandparents of the grandparents: he knew
everything, he knew life, death and miracles of gener-
ations of people from Polignano. He told me that for a
certain period he had run the risk of becoming mayor,
but then he had preferred the tranquillity of his coun-
tryside, of his almond trees which when in bloom were
a splendour, of his garden with tomatoes and potatoes,
carrots. and fragrant herbs.

Between land and sea, I don't know what intrigued
me more. I learned a lot more from my grandfather
on those morning escapades than from being bored in

class. This is how I spent my days while mom was at school. My father, on the other hand, with the excuse that my whims and my vain madness were affecting his mental health, finally did what, maybe, he should have done a long time before: moving to Bari, leaving me and mom. Officially because of me, actually because of another woman. Cetta and Rosella, my mother's longtime friends, the only people besides grandmother Nenetta and grandfather Giuseppe who tolerated me and I liked as well, had told them: «*da quanne ha murte Pite, ancaure neu sté sinde u fite?*—from the time Pietro died, only now do you smell the stench?" It was to say in Polignanese: do you know how long these facts have been known? Did you discover them only now?

It is true, however: not all evils come to harm us. After their separation, we put in more colour, both me and mom, like goldfish, which when you look at them through the bowl look even more colourful than they really are. We had resumed breathing freely, without having dad breathing down our necks. His always destructive criticisms, his contempt for us as if guilty of who knows what inexplicable wickedness.

After he left, we resumed searching for neuropsychiatric doctors and neurologists, looking for someone good to give us acceptable explanations for my strange behaviour. One, in particular, struck us, with his less destabilizing diagnosis than the previous ones. Finally, he seemed to have framed my main problem: high cognitive potential.

"It's not a bad thing, Nina!" he told her in a too confidential tone, rereading my answers to his questions.

"But it is not positive to have an IQ of 168," he specified, considering my difficulties in relating to others. "Paradoxically, despite being a genius she will always have difficulty in school." He advised her to talk to the director of the school I was attending, and she made an appointment right away.

"Maybe! Perhaps by moving her ahead in school, she will be able to find some topic that intrigues her! We will submit her to the entrance exams to check her level of knowledge."

Ten sheets, including questions and exercises that I had to solve within five hours, in the presence of seven teachers I had never seen. I answered those silly questions without any errors in eighteen minutes and twenty-two seconds, in front of incredulous eyes mixed with envy and fear.

In January, I went to the fifth grade when I was six years old. My classmates, however, were ten. Anagraphically and physically smaller than them, intellectually I was much more advanced. This meant always coming home from school with bleeding knees or scratched palms: it was nothing new to me, who had always been awkward in my movements. But if before I had been the torturer of myself, now I had become the conscious victim of shoving in the street or tripping in the corridors, of tugging at the school uniform that tore out pockets and blew off buttons; "*L pagghizz russ*", my red hair, was often castrated of entire locks by the teacher, when she could not, in any other way, detach the chewing gum that classmates stuck on it.

For grandfather Giuseppe, who came to pick me up at the exit, it was painful every time. He took it out on mom, who according to him did not impose herself on the director. It was not true, however: when she went to complain to him, the story was always the same. He laconically told her: "We have no special classes in which to insert her. Besides, why should we? Your daughter is a genius, she is not mentally retarded and we do not have teachers prepared to handle these situations. Professor, you know it better than me!"

She blatantly replied: "If I were in your place, I would know what to do!"

Their words, however, remained such, even if recited under the cowardly gaze of the other teachers present at the show, who, however, went to hole up in the safety of their classrooms with their normal children.

I always returned to the same class, with the same bullies. I did not understand the reason for their reactions to my questions or to the explanations I gave in place of those who should give them; I was unable to react by using the same weapons, totally disarmed and compliant to the point that I punished myself with studying, not realizing that it was my abilities, my memory and my skills that frightened others. The cuddles of my grandparents were worth nothing. They were very happy with my excellent scholastic results, despite everything: I was promptly excluded from everything and everyone, and I just couldn't stand it.

"But why, grandfather, am I invisible to the whole world? Why do they only talk to me in class when they

need my help?" I asked him with my eyes red with anger and pain, trying to stem the flow of those tears
that so much wanted to get out but should not do so,
because "You go to church to cry," my father said.

My insignificant physicality was a fact. Discrimi-
nating evidence. If, however, I had been truly invisible,
perhaps the others would not have targeted me: I could
have looked at them and satisfied my desire for knowledge and they would no longer have made fun of me.
I had therefore set myself the goal of weighing nothing and nothing I had come to weigh. I had become
anorexic, not understanding the far more invasive consequences of not eating.

When I crossed the threshold of the *medie*, junior high school, near my house, I was not yet eight
years old and I weighed no more than twenty kilos.
My grandfather had also become anorexic with me, as
he couldn't understand what was happening to me; he
tried to buy things I liked and he let grandmother cook
them, but I, after having swallowed everything reluctantly, went to "return" it to the bathroom with interest.
I had become very good at it.

I didn't last long in that high school either. Bullying
was the same everywhere I went, maybe it got worse.
One day at recess, I was surrounded by a bunch of
girls who had shoved me and jerked me really well,
bouncing me from one to the other, enough to tear
that black bat school uniform that I hated so much,
and then they said to me: "The world would be a better
place if you weren't there! When do you leave the face
of the earth?"

At that precise moment, I realized that maybe there was really something wrong with me. After all, I didn't have the habit of saying things that weren't true, so why should they? I was aware enough to understand that I was wrong, that my fallacious behaviour was the strange iceberg of something else, but I still didn't know what, just as the doctors who kept visiting me didn't. Everyone had their own opinions, without even knowing what they were talking about. So, amidst the hallucinated glances of the teachers and a series of other strange happenings in the corridors of the school, mom decided that I would continue studying at home with a private teacher. And so it was.

After junior high school, given my propensity for archaic languages, she then decided that I would attend the *liceo classico*, classical high school. It would certainly have taken less time if I had continued to study at home as I had been doing for junior school. Mom, however, had forced me to finish high school in the canonical times because, if from the point of view of school preparation, I was ahead of the others, psychologically I was still immature: I had to grow up, learn to relate, and I could only do it if I was among others. Even with a thousand risks.

As I started attending the first year of the *liceo classico*, my parents officially divorced. Those were strange years. I often discovered my mother worried in front of the news: she almost reminded me of her husband, when he talked about the railways and the political intrigues that revolved around us. Politics, which was the topic of discussion par excellence, was taboo for me, and not because I did not understand its meaning; on the contrary, the ubiquitous Dutiful-Oli dictionary omnipresent on my desk in my room or on school desks was always exhaustive in this sense. I, who had in mind all the events and developments and dates and statistics, did not really understand the meaning of "doing politics". Every day there was news of a new attack: industrialists, policemen, magistrates or barracks were the conscious or unwitting targets of a small group of people whom they called, at times, right-wing extremists, at other times, left-wing extremists. To me, they were the same thing. Bullies who targeted defenseless characters like me. People of culture who became the object of exploitation.

It had already happened a couple of times that some classmates had denied me school entry, "because there is a strike!" Strike for what? What did we, silly students of a provincial high school have to do with the power struggles or with the attacks, with politics? I was very scared on those occasions, and I accused mom of leaving me in the hands of the Red Brigades. She didn't left me alone since. I endured five long years doing this, with her accompanying me every day and picking me up from school.

I have some good memories of that period, always affected by depression and anorexia that continued swinging to afflict me. I managed to bond with some classmates. There were four of us, pestiferous and restless, the terror of the professors. We enjoyed ourselves like crazy and deep down we really were crazy, in our own way. Perhaps the driving force was me, who gave the "the" to pranks and spiteful acts, while the others, emboldened by my presence, took advantage of it: I was tolerated only because, in the meantime, my mother had become the principal of the same high school that I attended and from which I graduated in July 1979.

In September I enrolled at the university. We needed a special "dispensation" to register, since I was still a minor and therefore under the tutelage of both parents, at the behest of I don't know what kind of judge, who had established it without taking into account my volition. Not to mention that I hadn't seen my father for nearly ten years. Obviously, I had read a lot of judgments on the matter: I knew more than either of the biased lawyers. Maybe even the judge.

I had chosen the faculty of Ancient Letters and Philology. None of my high school friends had enrolled in that faculty, even though it was the most obvious outlet after classical high school. In those years, political science or law was in vogue; many had taken a sabbatical or had chosen to go to work in completely different sectors; someone had taken Medicine and Surgery, following in the footsteps of his father or mother, otherwise, he would not have had an easy time, in the faculty and at home. After all, I too had followed in my mother's footsteps.

My faculty was based in the Ateneo, in Bari, near the railway station. I had learned to travel by train: I went there alone and remained so as I followed the lessons, literally snubbed by the "colleague" students, envious of the influence I had over the professors.

The reasons were obvious to most, but not to my supposed peers.

At the suggestion of my mother and the university tutor they had assigned me, I never discussed the subject of age with anyone: I always kept it vague, never showing the university booklet, on which was written the date of birth. I had begun to dress in a more staid fashion and made up my eyes and mouth lightly. I didn't like myself so dressed up, but I seemed more credible in the role of university student, so much so that I had even started getting my first party invitations, all declined. Indiscriminately. Of course, I still happened to stumble alone or fall down the university stairs, by force of circumstances or because of someone else; I never remembered who that someone else was, so I could convince myself it was my fault.

"*Occhi non vede/Cuore non duole.*" "Eye does not see/heart does not hurt," I always said to grandfather Giuseppe, even though I did not really understand its meaning; I liked the sonority of that sentence, so much so that I had learned to enunciate it at the right moment. My self-esteem, in those moments, collapsed disastrously. When I managed to talk about it with my mother or grandfather, they always told me the same thing: that I had to evaluate things for myself and decide whether to continue to mortify myself and accept that others copy my notes or the translations in exchange for my acceptance, or continue to maintain my rigour and thus look in the mirror without being ashamed of myself.

I did not share the parasitic behaviour of my university colleagues: it did not seem possible that they did not have the same desire to learn or improve themselves. I was stubborn to defend topics that were difficult for most people, but extremely fascinating for me, not to show off, but just to measure my ability and surpass myself. To convince me that I was better than I saw myself. And I always saw myself as imperfect. The outlines of my personality were imprecise, full of smudges and therefore subject to maniacal correction. When someone, thinking of giving me advice, said to me: "Alina, be clever!" I was even more exasperated because I wanted them to give me precise instructions on how to become one. I also asked, curious: "Why? How do you get clever?" But no one committed themselves to any reasoning with me that made any sense, no one knew how to answer me. It was a concept beyond my reach. I took things literally, so I preferred to continue pretending to be stupid, so as not to rip or get ripped off.

When I was fifteen my real life began. Everything I had been before was confined to a glass bowl, like the limited world of a fish stolen from its ocean. Those were the years of the Ustica disaster and the Bologna massacre, outrages against public intelligence, mysteries never solved. The years of the earthquake in Irpinia, of Umberto Eco and *The Name of the Rose*, the assassination of John Lennon, the Moscow Olympics, house parties, for those who could afford them but also for those who could not, with a DJ and vinyl records,

the Spandau Ballet and slow dances. Nobody could
or should have refrained from showing and showing themselves off, at the risk of exclusion from the
elites and the spoiled habits, poison of my sold-out
adolescence. Those were the years of well-being, winter white weeks in the mountains and summers at the
lido seaside because even going to the free beach was a
declaration of a proletarian social status that just didn't
have to concern you; the years of Naj-Oleari designer
clothes, El Charro belts, disco and Timberlands. Those
were variegated years, with a thousand facets: there
were punks, goths, lovers of poet songwriters, heavy
metal or Lionel Richie's disco music. There were those
who chewed a little English and were therefore considered holders of absolute knowledge, as if it were the
Esperanto of the only possible universe, which they
then used only to repeat the same refrains of the same
songs. We boasted of being different from "those" who
had preceded us only because we believed we had to
take different paths, different from the snarling, con-
frontational and communal ones of the past years. We
felt genetically modified to compete and do better
than others.

III.

I was not like them. I was naïve. Out of place
wherever I was, small from the point of view of
age in an imperfect world made up of immature
adults. I was a grown woman and a child at the same
time: self-centered, stubborn, arrogant, insatiable and
very curious all at once; petulant, annoying, controversial and aggressive or very sweet, in a spit of seconds. I
surgically dissected everything around me, even what
did not concern me directly, and I still bear the marks
of this in my soul; I remember all the scars individu-
ally, which I could define temporally, so as to put them
back perfectly in their context. Too bad, however, that
I always and only saw myself in an apparent visibility
that excluded everything else.

It was precisely in one of my moments of apparent visibility that I met Nicola. It was a birthday party.
One of those snobbish parties to which they invite
everyone, even the most wretched, just to make up
the numbers, "otherwise the party won't be as good
as it should!" It was also for this reason that I always
declined all the invitations that, despite myself, were
starting to arrive. The birthday girl was called Marina:

she was enrolled in the same faculty as me but she had never interested me, and only for this reason she was already more likeable to me than the others. She had sent me the invitation at home, so I had no plausible excuses for mom. She was pleasantly surprised by the invitation and went gung-ho, imagining me totally re-sized in real life. Maybe with a guy to hang out with or go to the movies or dance with. A "normal" girl, though normal in mediocrity. I had tried to explain to her that it was not what she thought, that they had invited dogs and pigs and therefore I was just a number to make numbers.

"Dogs and pigs? But do you at least know what that means?" she asked me, knowing that it was one of those clichés that I had never understood, despite having learned to place it at the right moment.

They had really invited dogs and pigs to the party: the room had to fill up, otherwise it wouldn't be the party to talk about for days. I would have been a fish out of water, I would have floundered until I was exhausted. She, at least she, should have known. Mom knew me. She, on the other hand, told me: "Be clever, Alina. If you don't go there this time, no one will ever invite you again!"

My grandparents had repeated the same thing: it seemed that they all reasoned with the same head, which, however, was not mine. For that occasion, Mom took me to the trendiest boutique in Bari, because it was a must for me to wear a dress that they had never seen on me before. It wasn't even a Sunday or a good party. She had been helped by Cetta and Rosella. She already knew that she would not have patience if we went alone, and she was "equipped" for the afternoon of passion. I remember her withering looks, the only display she allowed herself in public when she disapproved of my behaviour or talkative arguments. As usual, I started with my long discussions on how one fabric was different from the other or on a fold that I didn't like or a lack of colour instead of many colours, so much so that the saleswoman had run out of her samples. They were all there, the clothes, displayed on the table waiting for my choice. In the end, I capitulated. I chose a rather strange Vivienne Westwood dress, a mix of punk and lace in an indefinable colour, between black and brown, which highlighted my waist and shoulders, even the red of my hair. It camouflaged my anorexic body perfectly as well. But that didn't deceive Nicola.

He intrigued me for his withdrawn manner; he seemed almost as much a pariah as I was. We were the only ones to stay on our own on the veranda when delirium was all around us. *Video killed the radio star* and *My Sharona* going wild with psychedelic volumes, ghostly lights that appeared and disappeared like blades to cut through the darkness of the evening and the green of the meadows. He was there, looking abandoned in a corner, leaning against the balustrade, smoking. He seemed to be looking at everything and nothing in particular. He had not even noticed my presence, a sign that I was not invisible only to myself. He turned to look at me but then went back to staring into the void again. He seemed to me like a puppet on a music box, one of those with a spring-loaded neck

that retracts on itself as you move it and then leans
over again and returns to its place. He inhaled and ex-
haled the smoke almost instantly, stopping to look at
the cloud that he had generated, in a strange way of
enjoying that incorporeal ascent to heaven, as if it were
his last cigarette before the gallows.

"It will seem strange to you but it's the first cigarette I smoke, maybe the last," he told me at a certain
point, as in the comic books, with the characters'
thoughts flowing indistinctly from one to the other in
a handful of pencil strokes. He threw his cigarette off
the porch, after looking that no one was passing by,
and the white cloud had suddenly dissolved. I got up
and joined him.

From a distance, perhaps because of how he was
dressed or because of his long hair, he seemed to me a
contemporary of my classmates. He had a barely visible beard, perfectly uniform from wherever one looked
at it. His indigo-coloured eyes were crinkled all around
by small wrinkles. If I had seen them on my father's
face, I probably would have told him he was old. On
him, however, they were of an absolute charm.

"Nicola," he said, holding out his big hand. "You?
University student like Marina, my niece?"

I looked at him with interest; it hadn't even occurred to me to explain other things to him.

"Yes, same faculty! My name is Alina," I replied,
pretending a detachment that I didn't have. Then, almost dissociated from myself, I heard my voice asking
him if I could stroke his beard.

He looked me straight in the eye. "Go ahead!" he replied laughing. And I was surprised to reach out to that short hairless space that had that silky certain don't know what of small children, mixed with a musky and wild smell that drew me to the innermost bowels. It reminded me of that French actor that my mother adored, and that she always went to see at the cinema with Cetta and Rosella. I think his name was Alain Delon. When they came back, they did nothing but gossip about him.

We started talking about topics that I liked. Stars— the sky was full of them that evening—with visible and invisible constellations; of climate, geography and strange countries, which he had visited in person and which I had only studied in books; of mathematical sciences and theories, of Latin and Greek and writers we both liked. We talked all evening. A couple of drinks, I presume alcoholic, that I hadn't had the courage to refuse had unleashed my long-windedness, but he didn't seem bothered, on the contrary! He kept listening to me, interrupting the flow of my words from time to time, but only to keep up with me.

"You know …" he told me at one point, "I imagine you are a perfectionist. But even bones weigh!"

I looked at him dazed, hungry for answers, curious to know how he had guessed my problem.

"Even if you had no fat or muscle left, you would still carry the weight of your bones on you. You could never weigh nothing, not even when dead, so make an effort to eat!"

He seemed really sincere to me. His eyes showed a healthy attraction towards me: they emanated almost the same aura that Grandfather Giuseppe had when he looked at me trying to understand what was going through my head. I was atavistically hungry for someone who took a serious interest in me: not for physical beauty, which was undeniable, but for all the potential and oddities inherent in my strange way of being.

He asked me a thousand and one things and I answered him, a thousand and one times. We talked for hours as if we had known each other for a lifetime and not for much less. It never occurred to either of us to delve too deeply into our age or social status. It was he and I, and that's it. Two entities in their own right, essential to each other. He was upset when they called me to leave. He kissed me softly on the cheeks, holding my head in his hands as if I were a porcelain doll to be handled with care.

The following Monday I found him outside the university. I recognized him right away. He was beautiful. More than one student had stopped to look at him but he had only had eyes for me. I smiled at him, and I greeted him with a wave of his hand. "Marina didn't come today," I told him from afar as he approached. He caressed me looking at me with his sweet eyes, then started to laugh. "I know, I didn't come for her!"

I looked around and he was alarmed. "Are you waiting for someone?" he asked me cautiously. I shook my head at him. Then he took the bundle of books from my arms and headed to a car in front of us. He opened the door for me as if it were the most natural thing in this world, and he motioned for me to sit down. I didn't think twice about it.

I let myself be carried away by his words as if they were fragments of lines to be stitched up to embroider new designs, and he had driven to the sea shore before I even noticed. I was totally in love with his way of doing and being, mesmerized by my reflection in his Ray-Ban glasses, infatuated by his hunger to listen.

"I wanted to breathe you," he told me after having parked the car in a small piazza on the seafront and came close to my neck with his nose. Then he made himself comfortable and started playing with my one hundred and two freckles—he counted them one by one—with my hair, his fingers combing them in a gesture of absolute intimacy that I had never shared with anyone, not even with my mother. Whom I forgot to warn about being late. Later, I told her that I had stopped by Marina to give her my notes because she had not come to class. I was all anxious as to why I hadn't warned her of the delay, but she didn't notice it, too happy that I was integrating into the "normal" world. Did she think I was finally growing up? Or was it she who got tired and was starting to let go of the reins with which I had tied her up until then? Who knows … maybe I had become clever at last. I invented a thousand commitments, new friendships or old friends from school, non-existent appointments and sudden lessons, everything just to be alone with Nicola: I had never felt for anyone what I was feeling for him. I had finally found someone, other than grandfather, able to spend whole afternoons with me just watching clouds or blades of grass grow, listening to the wind or enjoying the saltiness on their face. Someone who made me laugh and cry together and who was able to make me like even that life that until then I had preferred to avoid. That week was followed by many others. And many other lies that I called "for a good reason". I finally felt at peace with myself and with the whole world.

We started making love. He took me for the first time on the sofa at his home in Bari, while we were looking together at a book in archaic Latin that he had brought me from Rome. He was very sweet. He believed I was faking my inexperience when I really was inexperienced. He was the first for me. His caresses were pleasant to me, even when he pushed himself into me, where not even I had ever reached. When I started bleeding, I was scared: the blood always had a certain effect on me, especially for that iron smell that had bothered me from the first time I had menstruated. At first, I justified myself to him thinking I had my period early, but when I told him, he laughed because he understood. He hugged me protectively, almost fatherly, as if I were a small child, and languidly stripped off the only clothes left on me. He picked me up, carried me to the bathroom and gently washed the blood off. I let myself be pampered by his gestures and afterwards everything was easier. He took me again and then again, each time different from the other.

And when he was satiated, he held me between his legs to listen to me speak: while doing so, he continued to stroke my red hair that I had decided to straighten since he said he liked it better like that, so tamed.

I had changed and no one had noticed. Not even my mother or grandfather Giuseppe, who knew me well, although the feelings of guilt that followed the escapades forced me to have more compliant and reserved attitudes than my norm. It seemed that I had broken my crystal ball, selling off my integrity to come to terms with the common morality. Nicola had told me he worked in Rome: he was a senator. When I told him I had never seen him on the news, that I actually hardly saw him at all, he was amazed. He told me that he had many economic interests in Bari and that he would have liked to see me and be with me every time he came down from Rome. I would find him outside the university; he came to pick me up each time in a different car and each time he had a different explanation. He was paranoid, he told me then, he felt spied on, sometimes he had been caught by photographers and wanted to avoid these experiences for me. I did not mind it: I felt like the protagonist of a romance novel, at the center of a game of hide-and-seek with very specific rules.

"They should not see us around together," he said to me, "otherwise I wouldn't be able to come to you anymore!" I was afraid of losing him, so I indulged him.

The afternoon that I discovered it, I was at the hairdresser's taming my curls. I was leafing through a glossy magazine with lots of photos and gossip. There was an article about him and a photo that showed him

hand in hand with his wife and children next to him:
the boy like him; the girl a worthy replica of Barbie
who was next to him. And I had always hated Barbies.
The reporter wrote about the results of a motion in
the Senate attributed to him; there was a whole series
of reflections on his political activity, the same politics
that I had never understood in its entirety. "Careful,
Barbie is a *brigantista*, a member of the Red Brigades,"
I wanted to tell him. Then, in the caption that accompanied the photo, I read his age: fifty.

"As old as my father!" I said aloud. "It's not possible
… thirty-five years older than me!" I was petrified, only
a slight tremor in my hands and lips betrayed my anger. My helplessness. When I started breathing again
and looked in the mirror, it seemed that all the one
hundred and two freckles on my face had flown away.
I was suddenly out of breath again. No one had noticed that I was floundering, like a whale that has lost
its ocean course and finds itself beached in a cove, in
shallow water, stranded on the sand. In search of its
sea. Or its glass bowl.

I began to hold him off, with the excuse of exam
sessions and study. I began to skip lectures and university, our primary meeting place. I had anorexia come
back on me with a thousand other ailments inside.
One day, Nicola showed up at the front door of my
house in Polignano. He dragged me into his car. He
was pissed at me but I was more pissed than him: I had
my good reasons, and I threw them up on him, as I did
with food. He knew very well that he had deceived me.

He fell silent. Then he insisted. A lot. He apologized. And I wasn't good at denying myself to him. I was unable to find the magic wave that made me return to my glass bowl. When you discover the open sea, despite its dangers, you can't do without it. You can't help but breathe, and I started doing it again.

He had rented a villa in Cala Corvino, inside an expensive complex with a concierge. He generously rewarded the doormen of the two shifts and they closed their eyes and mouths when they saw us coming. We went there every time he came down from Rome. Sometimes we stayed there for hours, sometimes just a few minutes: it was our living space. Sex was not the only thing between us: there was complicity, play, the study of ourselves and the whole world, cuddles but also arguments, though futile. I was a sponge. And he played with it, with my obsession with studying matters further. Together we ranged from astronomy to geopolitics, from chemistry to molecular cuisine: his charisma and his culture were remarkable and intrigued me even more because they challenged me. He continually rewarded me with his pearls of wisdom; he nurtured my self-esteem by telling me that in life I could do whatever I wanted; he was amazed by my continuous desire to learn about new topics, which when we met again after a few days were already part of my pool of knowledge. I hadn't told him about my school background, my alleged schizophrenia and my IQ, or my very particular way of being, which nevertheless he liked. Above all, I hadn't told him about my real chronological age, even if one afternoon, talking about Marina's birthday, he asked me when it was mine. He was shocked when I told him I was born on January 1st, seconds after midnight. I was wrapping up on the year I was born when he told me: "Fuck! I too was born on January 1st!" Persistent, his belief that I was as old as Marina.

When I missed my period for the third month in a row, I began to worry. I hadn't told anyone. I had always been on time until then, never missed a monthly appointment. I had begun to write down all the discomfort, the strange sensations that I felt and that I had never experienced before. That Friday I told him. He was not a little alarmed. I saw him darken. The next day he had already gotten a test from the pharmacy. After reading the instructions, I peed on it in the bidet of our refuge.

The result was more than obvious. When I came out of the bathroom and held out the stick, his arms fell. He had looked at it several times, incredulous.

"Fuck! Fuck! Fuck!" He sat up, his head in his hands. I had never seen him so pissed off at himself before. He kept repeating that it shouldn't have happened, that it couldn't have happened to him, not then. I had sat in a corner, on the sidelines, letting him vent all his anger. I was not contemplating his desperation; it seemed that the consequences were all for him, only for him. Maybe I was an actress with a secondary role? When he finally looked up, he saw me staring at him with no expression whatsoever. I didn't expect him to react like this, I had regressed to my usual levels of emotionlessness. I got up without making a noise and just as silently I exited from that house and from his life.

IV.

I F THEY HAD ASKED ME to describe my feelings of that day, I would have read myself in the photo of a chair: insignificant and silent, with a straw seat and a very common backrest, made of two thin wooden boards and four legs; on those thin boards a scarf, forgotten by a distracted passer-by, which lets itself be whipped by the imperious wind and a thousand sand needles; in perspective the steep cliff, grim guardian of a stormy sea, and me, a shoddy presence waiting to welcome someone or something that would anchor my precarious presence, albeit at the mercy of that unlikely ground. Breath and longing of malicious waves that continually modify the shape, in an incessant mutation of colours and scents, so that every day offers a different sensation from the previous one.

I decided that the next day I would tell mom. But it was not possible. That night grandfather Giuseppe died. Silently, suddenly. With eyes watery from tears, mom filled a suitcase with whatever we could have needed. We would sleep at grandma Nenetta's for a few days. "The time to organize the funeral and fix a few things," she said. Instead, three days later grandmother had also gone, while we were still at her house: her heart had not withstood the pain. Mom exhausted her reserve of tears; she cried for her and for me, who was not able to shed a single one, not even for grandfather Giuseppe. Grandmother Nenetta had given mom the *coup de grace*. She had spoken to us for the last time the morning grandfather died when we arrived at her house. She had hugged us tightly on the doorstep, because inside, in the bedroom, were the funeral directors.

"The *tavutàri* are dressing him for the last time," she told us. She then took me to the kitchen, letting my mother go to say hello to her father for the last time. There were already a lot of relatives, cousins, brothers-in-law, nephews and nephews of grandchildren, old friends and Don Vito, the local parish priest. He hugged me. "You have to be strong," he told me, "You are a woman, stay close to your mother and your grandmother!"

But what could he know about my "being a woman"? Only Nicola really knew me! I broke away from his embrace and shrugged my shoulders. I suddenly felt alone, of that most devastating loneliness because it happens when you are not really alone. You realize it and you make it weigh you down when there are people next to you who look at you without seeing you, hear you without listening to you, judge you without knowing you. I felt suddenly and desperately alone. I, who was born already accustomed to being alone. I was lost to them.

* * *

I caressed my belly looking for comfort in that little creature that was hidden there, then I went to hide in my room: there, in the lap of my window overlooking the sea, I calmed down. Curled up like a hedgehog in the embrace of my grandmother's blanket, I drew away. Locked up in a world that was no longer mine alone, talking to that little creature I already called Matteo. I was sure he was a boy. I talked to him and he answered me. He described his amniotic cave to me, dark but warm, soft and comfortable. I sent him back my memory, what I had tried to explain to others so many times and as many times I had disavowed in words. Because no one understood. Certain sensations were not easy to understand.

I hadn't heard Grandma Nenetta speak since that short sentence on the doorstep. She had closed herself in her silent pain, with her black clothes perhaps too elegant for the occasion, but that was the custom then. With her green eyes suddenly turning brown beyond the lenses of her glasses. With her now orange hair streaked with white and her hands bruised from her gnarled wrinkles. Those same hands that cooked for me. Who hugged me and played with me. She had limited herself to hugging all those who had passed in procession in front of grandfather's coffin. He inside, strangely small, became a child in size again, with the rosary in his hands and the good suit. "The one he wore at my eldest daughter's wedding," said Mariuccia, the lady who for some time had been looking after them and their home. She was more devastated than my mother, who proved to be detached and the proud lady of the house and situation. Because behind the organization of a funeral there is a whole basic preparation that requires attention and knowledge of traditions. Starting with the death announcement posters and ending with the choice of music and songs for the mass. From the arrangement of relatives in the pews in the church to the choice of wreaths and cushions. From the choice of niches in the cemetery to the marble for the tombstone and the words to be engraved on it.

"Thank goodness we already have the family mausoleum!" mom said to everyone. "Because otherwise who would have given us the niche, with the overcrowding that exists?"

On that pitch dark night, I remained sleepless. I listened to the litany of the rosary on one of the sofas in the good living room, in the dim light of the fake candles on either side of the coffin, with my favourite blanket around me sitting next to my grandmother. From time to time, in dribs and drabs, someone would get up to go and eat something, drink a coffee or chat with those in the other rooms, who didn't feel like staying with the dead but couldn't help but stay. From time to time, someone lost the thread of the rosary, letting out a snore of exhaustion, so sudden and noisy that it suddenly awakened him. From time to time, grandmother Nenetta would get up, dragging herself heavily with the aching bunions up to the coffin, to look inside in the hope of catching a glimmer of life that was not there. From time to time, they knocked on the half-open door for a coming and going of cappuccinos and croissants offered to "console" close relatives. We returned from the cemetery when it was almost noon. The morning was clear with cold, swept by the mistral of the sea which gradually took away all the flowers from the wreaths, outside the family mausoleum. Mamma and Mariuccia had started to busy themselves with small chores around the house. There was food for at least eight days, so much stuff was brought in from everywhere to console us.

Grandma retreated to her room. I tried to be next to her when she went to bed. Although they had changed the pillowcases and sheets, the pillows still smelled of grandfather, with his odour of tobacco and wild musk that reminded me so much of Nicola's beard. I tried to hug her, to be close to her in my way as she liked it, but she turned the other away, on her side. When Mom looked out, she found me curled up against my grandmother's back as I was talking to her about Matteo.

"Whom are you talking to?" she asked me annoyed without even expecting an answer. "Be quiet and let Grandma rest!" She dragged me with her into that same good living room where you could never enter, "because you never know who can come and visit us, at least the good living room is always in order," they always said. And then they had opened it to make room for Grandpa's coffin.

"Stay with us to help us!" she told me, looking at Mariuccia dusting. We put back furniture and knick-knacks, in the vain hope of bringing things back to how they were three days ago, but three days were not enough to clear the air of the flower scents.

"Three days we mourn the dead," someone said cynically during the funeral, in the silence of the seconds preceding the priest's blessing. Mum also turned to look at who had uttered the sentence, but everyone had fallen silent. And on the third day, my grandmother was gone too. Just like that, in her sleep too, the best death, according to everyone. She hadn't risen from her bed of tears since grandfather's funeral: she hadn't eaten anymore, she hadn't spoken anymore, she had worn herself out, heedless of our appeals. Indolent and silent, she let herself die to chase, who knows where that dream that had lasted sixty years.

How far can a single moment be expanded? To enlarge an instant so that it can withhold everything, good and evil, bad and ugly, and finally seal it and forget it forever? I stood for hours looking out the window, on the edge of the walkable rocks. Sitting next to the patience of a solitary fisherman. Hugging my knees, I watched the glint of his nearby hook spinning in the bright glow of the slowly rising waves. He remained silent without even breathing, not a sound, not a breath until something at the end of the line manifested its tenacity of life with all the strength it was capable of. Then, and only then, did the fisherman fight. Just long enough to break that craving: he wrapped the reel quickly, with the fish wriggling on the salty rock, and before the last breath of life vanished, he unhooked it and threw it back into the water.

Why didn't this also happen to us, humans? With that "someone" who has captured us in body and spirit who, before our last breath, throws us back into the pit of life? In an awaiting, surprise, struggle and abandon to repeat itself. To infinity.

"Alinaaaaaaaa! Alinaaaaaaaaaaaaa!"

My mother's voice came amplified from the fireplace chimney. I wanted to close my eyes, and slip into the void without words, with soft and vague sounds like the undertow of the sea. I wanted to hold my breath but it wouldn't be enough. It wasn't going to make all the suffering go away just because that's what I wanted. A single wave is not enough to clean up the beach.

When I opened my eyes I saw her at the edge of the door, looking at me with a frown, in perfect coordination with the black clothing.

"What is it, Alina?" she asked me from afar. I remained motionless, as if invisible, I returned to observe the fisherman with the revived fish. I didn't answer her and she walked over. She stroked my silky red hair in such an unusual gesture that it made me jump in fright. I blushed with embarrassment as if she could have read my thoughts because at that moment I had thought of Nicola and that gesture that had been his first way of approaching me in intimacy.

"I have to tell you something," I told her then, continuing to look out the window at that precarious bait that glimmered among the swelling waves. She stroked my hair again, and that was just what I needed at that moment.

"I'm expecting a baby," I told her in one breath as if telling her more slowly could somehow affect her ability to listen to something that perhaps I should never have revealed. She started laughing. "What are you saying?" she replied amused. She repented immediately when she read my iron-gray gaze. "Sorry love, I didn't want to laugh. Where does this belief of yours come from?" she asked me, with the stunned expression of someone who has just heard a joke from someone from whom least expected. It was when I told her I took the test that she fell silent. She grabbed me by the shoulders and forced me to turn around, to look me in the face when I answered her. "What are you saying? What test?" she yelled at me in anger, her face red and her voice hoarse, broken in two by her nervousness. She went crazy at my half-hearted statements to her nagging questions, with the pressing evidence of her disbelief. I could not tell her everything, it was already too much for her and the burden on my conscience was too great; I could not tell her about Nicola, who could also be her husband and a father to me; I could not explain the subterfuges and lies, the announced escapes and her innocent distraction that had enabled me. She could not have understood that feeling, that gratification that came to me from the way he loved me.

"Love not love," Nicola called it. That all too evident feeling but to be kept hidden. One afternoon, after making love, he reiterated it to me: "I wish I could come out with you, but I can't. I wish I could get away from this story that makes me feel bad from feeling too good, but I can't. Our love is anachronistic, but it is real and lived. And it hurts me: do you understand, my little girl?"

I couldn't tell her about my disappointment. Of the fears that assailed me at night, mixed with the sweetness of his feelings. She wouldn't understand.

She slumped against the wall, letting herself slide to the ground. Her head between her knees massaging her temples with her fingers. Now and then she looked up and she stared at me as if she wanted to read inside me, inside that crazy head that had never stopped giving her problems, inside that too big heart in which she always got lost. But I was a wall of cold, impenetrable steel. She stood up laboriously. I heard her descend the stairs and arrive in the kitchen, with that chimney always too indiscreet to reveal every single movement, in the silence of that huge house now too empty. I heard her talking on the phone. After a few minutes, she reappeared like a shadow behind me.

"Put on your coat, let's go!" she said.

"Let's go where?"

"To a doctor friend of mine, in Bari," she replied. She drove strangely in silence, her gaze intently at the road now dark with the sunset. It took us less time to get to Bari from Polignano than to find a parking space for the car in the city center. We had cut via Sparano halfway at least a dozen times, then I remembered the garage where Nicola sometimes parked his car when he came to pick me up from university. The doctor's office must have been in that vicinity, we went around it.

"Go down to that garage," I said, pointing to the sign on the side. She looked at me dumbfounded, then she followed the arrow and slipped inside, continuing to glare at me as she braked on the ramp. "Leave it here, now the attendant is coming to get it," I said, opening the door as he arrived with his parking pad in his hand. "Good evening, Miss!" he said, amazed by my unusual company. Mom didn't speak to me anymore. She seemed lost in her thoughts, with the bewildered look of someone who has so many fears and doubts that she doesn't even know where to look.

The doctor's office was two blocks away. She announced our arrival on the intercom, and they opened for us immediately. She headed for the elevator and I followed her. It seemed such an unbearable distance, the one between the ground floor and the fourth floor, that when we went out on the landing, we both sighed loudly.

I had never seen that doctor. She shook my hand. "Hi Alina, don't you remember me?" I didn't answer her, wondering if I should have recognized her. Mom had withdrawn for a few minutes and then she reappeared with eyes swollen with tears and a reddened nose; she held out her hand to me and led me inside.

Loredana, the doctor's name, showed me a screen. "Take off your socks and panties," she told me, and so I did. Mom was amazed to see me so relaxed: she looked at me with a surprised face and with a nod she indicated that strange cot along the wall. I approached and the doctor helped me to climb on it. She placed my knees astride the stir-ups at each end. I looked at

Mom but she was looking away, standing in front of the window.

Loredana explained everything to me. She told me to call her that, before slipping a strange gloved contraption between my legs, inside me. With her hand on my slightly rounded belly and her gaze at the black and white monitor in front of me, she started moving that foreign body, as Nicola did when he was inside me while we were making love. It did not give me the same pleasure but I, for obvious reasons, refrained from telling her.

When Loredana called her, Mom approached: she looked at the monitor, then at her, then again at the monitor. Incredulously amazed by the size of that now fully formed creature, which she imagined still as an embryo.

"From his size and his penis, I'd say he's a fourteen-week-old male, Nina," Loredana told her as she set the images on photos that a strange printer beneath the monitor spat out in sequence.

"There are no problems of any kind!" she then said, turning her gaze first to me and then to mother, who had begun to cry in silence. She headed back to that window opened to the world, as if the darkness beyond the glass had been more comforting.

Loredana then went to listen to the runaway little heart. "You hear it, Nina!" she said amused to my mother who continued unperturbed to look out.

I dressed behind that screen while the two of them were talking. When I came out dressed, they both froze, as though alienated from my presence. "Can I talk to you alone for a moment?" Loredana told me, looking sideways at Mum waiting for her confirmation, that had arrived immediately. She rose from her chair before I even answered and went out, closing the door behind her. I sat in the same chair, still warm from her. Loredana took my hand.

"Don't worry, Alina! Now you have to be tranquil for yourself, your baby and your mom. She is angry now, but she will calm down. Children always calm grandmothers!"

I nodded calmly enough and she continued: "I prescribed folic acid for you, it is very good for him and we are already late. I usually prescribe it from the fourth week of gestation and you are more or less at the fourteenth. How long have you not had your period?"

I escaped her gaze. "Four months in two days."

"How long have you known you're pregnant?"

"We took the test the day before Grandpa died."

She looked at me in amazement. "We have?" she asked me taking my hands. She came closer. "You can tell me, you know?" she told me as her accomplice, "I'm not your mother, you can tell me! You know who the father is, don't you?"

I nodded without answering her and she pressed me.

"I can't say it."

She looked me in her eyes. "But you can tell me one thing … is it only one or more than one?"

I looked at her in horror and shook my head, but what was she thinking? "Of course it's one!" I answered immediately, and she breathed a sigh of relief.

"Your mother and I were afraid that you had been raped," she said then. She got up and opened the door for Mom. Without saying anything to her, she looked into her eyes and smiled at her.

V.

I N THE ELEVATOR, SHE LOOKED at me as one looks at a stranger.

"You're not my Alina anymore," she said, "when did I lose you? When did you grow up, that I didn't even notice it?"

I didn't answer her. I didn't know what to answer her. I wanted to tell her so many things. I would have had to explain too many things to her. She stopped in the doorway. She looked left and right, then she took me by the hand. "Let's go to the pharmacy in via Sparano, I think it is the closest."

And as we crossed the street hand in hand, I saw him. He was in front of us, on foot and alone. He was watching us. I hadn't seen him since the day we found out I was pregnant. The day I ran away from him. I involuntarily tightened Mom's hand and she stopped at the curb.

"What is it?" she asked me thoughtfully, turning to look at me. I looked away from him and shrugged. I absent-mindedly returned to look at him as he approached us.

"Nina ... is that you?" he said to my mother, she still baffled by my strange reaction. She took a second look at him, looked at him better. "But ... Nicola, is it really you? But ... how many years have we not seen each other?"

I wanted to sink to the ground. They kissed and hugged like two old friends, then she introduced him to me.

"Alina, he's an old friend of mine from school, Nicola." Then, turning to him: "She is Alina, my daughter!"

He reached out to take my hand, and he squeezed it while my mother pressed him with her questions. But what are you doing here in Bari? You know, I see you in the papers! But where is your wife? How beautiful, your children!

How many silly questions to listen to! How many obvious answers for him to give, in an unusual and absolutely unexpected context. Between one answer and another they decided to have a coffee together. She told him about her parents who had died suddenly three days after each other. He did not know and offered his condolences, sincerely sorry. He tried to extend his sympathies to me too, but I continued to walk beside them as if I were an automaton. I lined up the people we passed in a row like toy soldiers, with their empty faces and busy hands; I tried and tried to make sense of that silly walk. I kept walking beside them deaf and blind to their every call, joke or laugh. Armoured in my cold metal shield. Insensitive and distant from the two most important people in my life. Suddenly close but light years away from me.

It was when we sat down at the bar that they started talking about me. Nicola watched me attentively, perhaps ready to capture my every slightest and imperceptible reaction to that paradoxical situation. I pretended to watch elsewhere. I was a master at this, even with my ears straining to pick up every single word of theirs. At a certain point, as the coffee had turned into an aperitif, they started a discussion about their children.

"How old are your children?" Mom asked him. Nicola replied that he had a twenty-year-old son and one who would come of age shortly thereafter.

"Ah! So they are older than Alina!"

"What do you mean, older? Why? How old are you, Alina?"

I didn't answer him, but mom did it for me.

"Fifteen! It doesn't seem like it, does it? '

He looked at me like a blind man while Mom kept bragging about my superior intellectual status, continuing to show me off as a circus freak. I got up and went even farther than where I hadn't been. I went out into the street, leaving them inside, dismayed. I crossed the street and headed for the only empty bench in the garden of Piazza Umberto, crowded with caregivers of all nationalities, with their washed-out blond hair and miniskirts always too short, and street vendors with their wares on sheets covering the rough concrete floor, ready to run off when the police came to chase them. My mother, I was sure, would not come after me. Not anymore now. She knew me too well, she knew I needed to breathe deeply, with my mouth open. If I had been at school, I would not have been uncertain: I would have said to the teacher: "There, it's him! It was he." Pointing my accusing finger at Nicola. "He is the person who made me a woman, the father of the child I am expecting!" I would have told her. In other times. I was in that classic stalemate, that thin thread between heart and brain that has always de-stabilized my vital balance and forced me to make too partial judgments about others. If I had followed the brain, I could have silenced my conscience, rendered my morals whole and saved my injured dignity. I could have told the whole truth on the spot, with my main actors both involuntarily present and unaware of the epilogue. But they, my actors, how would they react? The scars of those behaviours of mine were still too fresh, in my heart and on the skin, irrational to others even if they were sensible to my way of seeing. How many times had I asked myself: "Why can't I think like the others, who have no qualms about deceiving? Why am I like this?"

I got up from the bench and walked back to the bar. I spied on them in the mirror in the front window. They were still there, but the scene had changed. He sat next to her, his tired hands between his legs and his long hair with whiter highlights—apparently drained; she, on the other hand, had her elbows planted firmly on the table to support her head in her hands, her fingers massaging her temples as she always did when she had some headscratcher to solve. Had they felt observed? They both turned to look at me as I quietly walked back into the bar. I had never been aware of visual expressiveness in others, and this was perhaps the worst of my difficulties in interpersonal relationships that I had found myself managing in my unmanageable life, until then.

My bewildered gaze lingered first in those cerulean eyes that had bewitched me with their magic, then in Mama's green ones, which were coloured anything but green. I could not understand what they wanted to tell me, neither one nor the other. I sat in front of them: I could have been anything at that moment. Leaf swept by the wind, severed from its branch even if immature in colour; cloth tied by too weak pegs, whipped by that same north wind, with the raised dust to smear it again; umbrella against the wind that bends with its ribs and turns back the dodged raindrops. I could have been anything but I was nothing.

He took his wallet from the pocket of the blue cashmere jacket that suited him so well. He peeked into it, into the small fold in the leather, pulled out a note and left it on the table. "Call me whenever you want," he told her, not expecting an answer. Then he got up and walked over to me, he kissed me softly on the forehead. "Take care of yourself, princess."

I stood looking at him until he disappeared through the door, out of my life again. I thought about the fisherman. To his patience tied to the line, with that nearby hook at the mercy of the waves to complicate his fishing; with those unaware fish poised between life and death that, in their longing for life, were able to look the fisherman in the eye and once again earn the longed-for liberation. I looked bewildered at my mother, her eyes too red that looked as brown as the mud that dirties the road, already dirty on its own, when it rains a lot. She got up. "Let's go home," she told me, taking my hand.

* * *

I found myself in Milan without realizing it. I had let the images run fast, sliding smooth as new oil on the marble of my heart. Like uncut film stills and mnemonic transcendences, the images: the patience of the fisherman, the rocks and cliffs, the waves on the breakwaters and the boats peeling from time and the sea, along the shoreline of the port. Parts torn from me like wide-angle panoramic shots fixed in the eyes, beyond the filthy glass of the train. I followed the trail of those tracks, crowded with old containers of souls crossing frantically, in their always too hasty getting on and off. And the imagination, laced with the gaze at the faded slides, had gone to that kite that soared along the fields, the rolling hills, the stripped trees and the bushes slapped by the wind. It had stopped at those sparse abandoned houses, with their stables in the distance and the sound of animals, only in memories. It was drowned in the sea of trebuchets whipped by the mistral, between Puglia and Molise, huge spiders planted in the crystal of the waters to act as fishing houses for land peasants not used to their navigation.

It had lingered in the long blades of fine sand that separated from the sea and the sky that single ridiculous skyscraper erected in front of the blue immensity, an insult to the heavenly natural splendour. The time of a blink of an eye and I reopened my eyes and we were already in Bologna. Torn too fresh, with the smell of death still on me and the fogged eyes of travelling spectators. It was a breadth from there to Milan. I hated the city immediately. It smelled of gray and industrious soot, of high-rise buildings soaring in the mist with ghostly lights on to serve as headlights in the darkness of an even darker night. It tasted of haste and carelessness, unpleasant sensations to the skin, ugly for that alone, even without any knowledge of the cause.

We had never been there, neither me nor mom. I didn't even know where the idea of going right there had come from. We could have gone anywhere; we were alone and so we would have remained. Alone even in flight.

All that had been needed was a chat at the hairdresser, shopping in the square or at the Thursday market. Everyone "knew". The rumours in the village had spread at the speed of light, for obvious reasons. First of all, the awareness that I was a minor and different from my peers, had paved the way for a whole series of assumptions: I had been placed on the scene of a gang rape, then within an orgiastic religious sect devoted to who knows what divinity, so I had been included in a circle of high-ranking prostitutes who granted their favours to university professors in exchange for promotions; for a few days there was even talk of incest, blaming my elusive parent who had never deigned to look at me in unsuspected times, let alone thereafter, with a bastard grandchild on the way. The spotlights had then turned on the only three Polignanese boys who attended the university in Bari, with whom I had found myself travelling from time to time on the train: they too, poor things, had been assailed by a thousand questions they could not answer. In the lotto betting that had arisen, of course, the unknown identity of the "culprit" had dominated, which mom had kept secret even from Cetta and Rosella, which was already an exceptional thing in itself. They too, who had always been more than sisters to my mother, knew nothing about it: it was then that they had moved away from us. Just when we needed them most.

Mother had turned to a trusted lawyer to whom she had told everything, even about Nicola. And he had advised her, for the sake of me and of the child who was about to be born, to leave Polignano, because there we would always be the subject of discussion and gossip; he had also secretly contacted the "alleged" father, to understand what his intentions were towards us even if, until I reached the age of majority, he could not do anything but risk jail for child abuse, as well as a divorce that would have seriously undermined his political credibility at probably the least opportune time. I had hidden in the house with my burden starting to become all too evident. I didn't want to leave, but it was the only sensible thing to do. I didn't have much choice. Shame was beginning to take the upper hand.

We left Polignano at night, like two thieves fleeing a crime scene before the alarm goes off and the police arrive. "Little luggage, we'll buy everything there!" she told me. When all was said and done. She had asked for a transfer for serious family reasons, accepting the compromise of going to direct a junior high school instead of a senior high school, but it was the only viable way in the middle of the school year, to be based in Milan and not in a village of the hinterland. I hated her at that moment. I had that absurd trip explained in great detail: timetables, trains, routes and cities that we would cross. Not that I didn't know, but school notions are always divorced from context and I needed certainties. Of days and hours that were "scanned" down to the smallest detail, because all the unscheduled ones continued to be unwelcomed.

I needed only a backpack for the memories. I had put in a few photos, the ones I liked best, with me as a child dressed in white and full of pranks, with sand in my mouth and shoes never on my feet: this was how I wanted to tell myself to Matteo. I had only put three books in them, those dearest to me, the ones I would read to him as soon as he listened to me when he would pop out of my shell. I had left everything else: I would not have been able to take the sea or the rocks and sand of Porto Cavallo with me, with euphorbia, broom and rosemary; the fishing boats in Cala Paura, with their nets soaked in seaweed and salt, small bream, thrushes and rainbow wrasse; lizards, hornets, butterflies or the brackish scent of multi-coloured carrots and potatoes when they first bloom with the smell of the ground still on them. It was all a vacuum, in my heart, like the universe around me. Mom didn't ask me anything and I didn't tell her anything. But it was all too obvious, even for me, someone who had no ability to read other people's emotions, the way she looked at me with different eyes. She was studying my renewed way of doing things, matured in some ways but compromised by fluctuating self-esteem, seriously dropping since Nicola was no longer close to me. She was trying to figure out how, where and when I had changed and why she hadn't noticed. She imagined everything without asking me anything, just fantasizing in my gaze. And in my silences.

Cold air enveloped us. Doubly cold compared to the spring sun we had left in Polignano the morning before. Molten steel and pungent ice and cartons on the ground to serve as makeshift beds everywhere. Dingy worn blankets over gaunt bodies even more worn and smelly. I had never seen such people in Polignano, not even in Bari when I was going to university. "But what are they doing on the ground, don't they have a home?" I said aloud in the taxi that was driving us to the hotel. The taxi driver had looked through the rear-view mirror with a gentle smile, "The street is their home," he replied with a strange accent. As if it were a normal thing, living on the street! He went back to looking at the road ahead, then he looked in the mirror again, first me and then Mom. "First time in Milan?" he asked her, lingering in my gaze as Mom answered.

"First time, yes! Moved here for work." They continued to talk and I definitively distanced myself, my gaze fixed on the road and my hand on my stomach, with the pouring rain that had begun insistently to drum all its anger on us. Not even Milan wanted us.

The hotel where he had accompanied us was very nice. It must have been in my mother's eyes too because I saw her astonished when the taxi stopped right in front of it. She gasped as the taxi driver unloaded our meagre luggage from the hood. It was barely dawning outside. The hotel porter was waiting for us. He motioned to a boy dressed as a tin soldier, who approached and loaded our two suitcases, all alone like us, onto a trolley that he pushed towards one of the elevators. Tired we followed him, our eyes lingering on paintings and chandeliers, gilded mirrors and vases full of flowers. I counted everything, in order not to think about anything. Light bulbs, magazines, armchairs, ashtrays … anything that could be measured with numbers, just to think of nothing else.

He accompanied us to the threshold of the door of our room, on the fifth floor. I didn't have time to undress before I was already asleep. Convulsive dreams entered my sleep. Empty pools, stairways reaching towards the sky, too long to climb, and damaged planes attempting makeshift landings right on my sea: different subjects for sequential dreams.

I woke up in a cold sweat in a room I didn't recognize. I looked left and right and felt alone. It was then that I "felt" him for the first time. It seemed that he, even in the water shell, had perceived my feeling of loneliness and wanted to give me a sign. A couple of little feet kicked me inside, and when I put my hand on them, they did it again. I'm not alone and I never will be, I thought at the time.

At the same moment, the room telephone rang intruding. I looked around to see where the source of that annoying malaise was. I saw it on the bedside table, on the other side of the bed. Mom wasn't there. I replied. It was the hotel switchboard.

"I'll pass you a call from Rome," she told me.

"Okay," I replied, waiting. I recognized his voice right away.

"Nina, are you all right? Have you settled down?"

I lacked the breath to answer him.

"Nina! Nina, is that you?" he continued from the other end of the phone. I called upon all my strength and said, "I'm Alina."

He answered after a moment as long as a winter. "Alina, my little one."

VI.

THE PHONE CALLS BECAME DAILY. As soon as Mom left for school, he called. Sometimes we talked for hours, sometimes for a few seconds. My knowledge of time has never been truly reliable. When I ended the phone call I started writing, thinking that I wanted to do it for the rest of my life, so many were the emotions that arose from those unspoken silences. My first novel was born this way: in the company of a son who, although not yet born, already gave me indications of life, listening to a love crystallized in the memories that gave me the strength not to drown in the sea of loneliness in which I had sunk. I missed Polignano. I missed it like the air, pregnant with salty clouds, crisp blue, smelling of water and undertow, and swollen waves with fish in the whirlwind of the carousel. Those walks in the alleys on Sunday morning were absences of the heart, between the time steps of flowered balconies and clothes hanging in the shade of the wind. Immense voids of children's memories, playing in the dunes, talking with crabs or starfish; everything had failed me except the memory, which I refreshed by telling Matteo, waiting to bring him there

in person. And to read him that novel, written with
him and for him. That story of the sea, of starfish and
mischievous fish, of dancing mermaids and thieving
octopuses, of magical sand and invisible rocks; of the
smell of seaweed and moss and nervous waves when
the evening was pitch-black night; of rainy clouds
and breathtaking blue skies, immersed in the majestic
depth of the water. I had never been good at drawing,
but it was easy for me to imagine and put funny, colourful and smiling fish on paper; comfortable rocks to
explore and beaches full of happy children under sun-
faded umbrellas, with mothers intent on collecting
scattered games and fathers intent on catching crabs.

Milan bothered me, with its catalogue of loneliness
and discouraged existences that dragged themselves
frantically into the whirlwind of life. I went out little
if I was alone: I could not get used to that noisy traffic, with the large avenues and roundabouts, cars, taxis,
trams and bicycles all together on the same routes at
the same time; I could not tolerate the noises of the
subway that rose from the underground too amplified
for my senses, like rash emotional earthquakes, and
left me with my heart in my throat and a faint voice;
I could not understand all those homeless people on
the street, distracted presences with their cardboard
blankets and the tin cans next to them, containers for
a few survival coins; I couldn't understand the gypsies
on the sidewalks, with their babies asleep in their arms
and people walking around them like ghosts with distracting thoughts. We stayed in the hotel for just under
a month, just enough time to fix the house that Nicola,

in agreement with my mother, bought for us without my knowledge.

It was a yellow-painted house with a railing running all across it, in the Brera area. My mother loved it right away: she said that she didn't feel as if she were in Milan, with those courtyards and those wrought-iron balconies, the human dimension of the chattering from one door to the other, the noises of appliances and the cats peeping out between the pot of geraniums and that of cyclamen. She thought of me when Nicola asked her for information on the type of property to buy. She was sure that I would have preferred to live there rather than in an anonymous block building, if not in one of the many skyscrapers that soared along the skyline of the city. She was sure that Matteo would be better too, in a place like this: he would have his courtyard to breathe in the green space, to enjoy the sun—when and if it peeked up—to learn to walk or ride a bicycle or play football with friends. She was planning my life as her parents had done with her. She had made clear pacts with Nicola, guilty unaware of having circumvented and made a minor pregnant; he had to stay on the margins of our lives but contribute to it more than effectively and, when I reached my age of majority, he should recognize Matteo, giving him his surname. She was blackmailing him.

I could see no further than my now deformed belly. I just thought of experiencing the sensations of his movements, his overbearing feet pointing to the wall of my belly, the excruciating back pain from the weight of two bodies in a skin that was no longer mine alone. I didn't think about the future. I would not have known where to start, with the baby and with the birth, and I was hardly self-sufficient, not even for my daily things. I had learned to cook by force of circumstance. There was no grandmother Nenetta to teach me how to make lasagna or eggplant parmigiana or mussel omelette, and mom went to work: so I had committed and, as usual, I had deepened my knowledge of the subject beyond belief, so much so that I became much better than mom. Maybe even grandmother Nenetta, may she rest in peace. Not only that, I also learned to cook the typical Milanese and Lombard recipes: *risotto* with *ossobuco*, fried meatballs, cutlet, *cassoeula* and sweet and sour pumpkin and many others, made with ingredients we had never used in Polignano. Strangely, I had begun to overcome my apathy for novelty, or perhaps it was the insights on the subject that intrigued me to the point of making me overcome the crises that had plagued me until then. Our sparse Milanese bookshop started to fill up with books from the most disparate topics, ranging from cooking to children, pediatrics to psychology. Dissertations on gynecology and the various birthing techniques had nourished my strong curiosity about how that puppy, in person, came out of my belly: after the initial discomfort, I set myself to look at things with the most aseptic eye possible, otherwise fear would have paralyzed me. Mom enrolled me in the prenatal course, at the hospital where I was to give birth; I met the gynecologist and the midwife, who had taken a liking to me despite all my problems. They told me in a very serene way what was going to happen, and how that moment would more or less reveal itself; they explained to me how to breathe in rhythm with the uterine contractions when they would arrive; they showed me many drawings that depicted the various stages of childbirth, with the changes that would take place in my body, from labour to expulsion of the fetus and placenta. Both had already had the opportunity to give birth to girls even younger than me; in my case, however, perhaps they would have some extra difficulties, in consideration of my sensory perceptions much more amplified than the norm. They even taught me to change the diaper or clean the delicate skin of babies, heal the umbilical cord until it fell out, and manage neonatal abdominal colic. I had to become a grown-up by force.

At the stroke of the seventh month, not a day before not a day later, mom and I went to buy the layette for Matteo: we emptied the Prenatal by buying everything, from intimate bodysuits to rompers, from leggings to tiny socks, from sheets to the covers, from the stroller to the cot and to the bag to take to the hospital, stocked with everything needed. On that occasion I was particularly calm: I did not have any kind of crisis, on the contrary, I sincerely enjoyed myself, anticipating the moment in which I would have that little creature in my arms that was beginning to feel a little tight in my belly.

It was during a furtive morning phone call from Nicola a couple of months later that the waters broke. There was an important discussion in the Senate, he was part of the commission that dealt with the bill

in question. He was more alarmed than I was: paradoxically, it was I who calmed him. Mom and I had
organized ourselves; I knew very well what I was going
to go through in a few hours; we had planned everything down to the smallest detail, otherwise, I would
have gone into confusion. Within an hour I found myself in the hospital, with my mother and midwife close
by and my belly full of cables tracing the vital signs of
that child who seemed to be in a hurry to look out.
I helped myself with the breathing techniques they
had taught me in the preparation course and I ignored
those devastating pains that ripped my stomach and
legs. I withstood the painful and ever more sudden as-
saults of his thrusts, and he peeped out claiming all the
anger and strength he was capable of. I had been very
good, at least until I heard him cry with all the breath
he had in his throat. I had not taken into account all
the cold that had enveloped me immediately after, so
strong that not even four blankets had managed to
warm me.

The silence had awakened me, I was alone in the
room. A dim light filtered through the window, it must
have been late afternoon and I was still cold. On the
table next to the window a bouquet of flowers, with a
note attached and a wrapped tray, perhaps sweets, had
reminded me of Matteo, but when I looked around, I
didn't see a cradle or anything else that spoke of him.
Yet I remembered having given birth to him: I remembered his crying, then nothing else. I tried to go back
to that moment with my memories, but the only thing
that I remembered clearly was that feeling of cold,

right after hearing him cry, that hadn't left me yet. That same cold would stay with me for years.

My mother organized everything with a coldness that matched the Milanese frost. The day my son was born, she demanded that Nicola leave the commission, in the Senate, to come to Milan to see his son, even from a distance, from behind the anonymous glass of the nursery, in a hit-and-run fashion that included to be accompanied to the Municipality to declare Matthew. For obvious reasons, Nicola would not appear on our family record; I was still a minor, under the exclusive tutelage of my mother, and Matteo, who had been declared the son of an unknown father, would have my surname. She hadn't wanted him and me to cross paths more closely. She did not know that when two souls are assonant, as Nicola and I were, even if they play different music they are always tuned to the same wavelength. I don't think she ever felt anything like this for anyone, maybe not even for my father; after all, I had never really explained my feelings towards Nicola and she had never asked me anything about it. In retrospect, I think she always thought that Nicola had seduced me, forcing me to have sexual relations with him, not realizing at all my consent to having it or the gratifying feeling of well-being, when I was with him.

What I felt when I was with him was not something describable. Our nakedness had never been measured in centimeters of uncovered skin, but in millimeters of soul in our eyes, all that flashed out of our eyes when we were close; all that transpired from the anxiety of our voices when we were on the phone. It was a love that created restlessness, without rules or certainties other than those related to the presence of both even in absence. No, I don't think my parents had ever experienced these feelings for each other: they were atheists toward the god of love. No catechism of any kind could ever lead them to the right path. Talking about it with my mother and not being understood, what sense would it make? In fact, I changed my mind about her when I saw her look with love at Matteo. He melted her like ice in the sun. He filed the hard shell and she returned light and mild as when I was little. Towards Nicola, however, she was inflexible: as long as I was under her tutelage, I would never have relations with him, even though he had admitted, albeit unofficially for the moment, his paternity. Besides, the similarity between them was too evident: the same lips and eye colour. He was blond like his father and not red like me.

It was my greatest terror, that he would be born a redhead: I already imagined the teasing he'd get at school. It was the first thing I asked Mom when I saw her return to the room with Matteo in the hospital cradle, before even checking if his fingers and toes were all there. If he had been red like me, he would have reminded me too much of Oronzo, my classmate in high school, who hadn't stood up to teasing and had committed suicide. His only fault, that of having red hair. When it had happened, this fact had rolled off my back: I had only talked about it with my grandfather

Giuseppe when the following Sunday we had gone to the cemetery to bring him some flowers. Grandpa then reassured me: "It's not the hair colour that made him do what he did," he told me while we were on his grave. Immediately afterwards, however, he had given himself a cough, to camouflage his weeping eyes with his handkerchief.

Who knows why memories always appear vivid when you least expect them? While I was thinking about Oronzo, it came back to me on a summer Sunday morning in Polignano. Maybe I was four. Mom and I were going to the grandparents' house for the usual Sunday lunch, without dad. We'd spent the whole short walk from our house to theirs arguing over the colour of my hair. She had told me that she too had red hair when she was little, but that when she grew up the colour had changed to a golden brown.

"But I want it to change now!" I shouted at her. "I want yellow hair like Raffaella!"

She had tried hard to muffle my tone, they were all looking at us in the street, but when we got home, I raced into the kitchen. I imagined that grandmother Nenetta was still cooking: I had brought my hair close to the fire under the pot of that ragù sauce which was supposed to simmer on Sundays. Grandmother, distracted by the preparation of the tiramisu, had smelled a strange odour of burning and she had thought of the sauce, but when she had turned to look at the pot, she saw my burning hair; she was frightened and shouted mom's and grandfather's names, who rushed to help her first and then me who, undeterred, looked defiantly at mom. My hair? From long they had become short, but their colour had remained the same.

While I was lost in memories, Matteo immediately attached to my breast. Even though his feeding sometimes hurt terribly, he left me with a feeling of eternity. For the first time in my life, I felt I was indispensable to someone, and it concerned me deeply: what if I hadn't been able to breastfeed him? Everyone could change diapers, even the boys, but milk and mother were irreplaceable. The first time they brought him to my breast, he explored me hesitantly, then he snatched at my nipple like a dog when he plays with a bone, with his tiny nose planted in the swollen breast, and seemed to hardly breathe anymore. In mutual distress, we had become one.

My hospital stay lasted very little: just two days and the three of us returned home. Matteo immediately proved to be a quiet child. Mom hired a nurse specializing in neonatology who would relieve her at home since she had to go back to work and she didn't trust leaving us alone.

"How could I be calm knowing that they are alone at home, both children?" she told Eleonora when she first came home. I was bothered by this total lack of trust on my mother's part: it almost seemed that she didn't want to see me grow up, even though in the meantime I too had become a mother. My face darkened but I did not reply, and Eleonora, who had noticed it, secretly winked at me. She, who was twenty-five, immediately took a liking to me. She wasn't as pushy as the others. The hospital nurses had all looked at me sideways and muttered; she was discreet and she trusted me, she especially let me take care of Matteo, helping me only when she saw me in difficulty or I asked her. Of course, she could not understand my seeming lack of expressed affection towards my son, but she did not know my previous history: she thought of a behavioural problem at the character level, perhaps exacerbated by the difficulties related to pregnancy and my situation as a single mother.

I was too technical and precise towards my son, it seemed that I did everything mechanically and not because my heart told me. Even in the management of typical abdominal colic or in weighing, before and after feedings. Or when the umbilical cord had fallen off: she had not yet arrived and I had managed by myself to disinfect and bandage Matteo's tummy under my mother's astonished eyes.

Nicola and I spoke by phone every day, always in secret. I mentioned our strange story to Eleonora, telling her what was tellable. Then, one morning, during one of our phone calls, Nicola told me that he wanted to see us, Matteo and me, that he wanted to stay with us for a while and that he would take advantage of his party's national congress to come to Milan. There and then I didn't know what to answer him. When I told Eleonora, she replied that she would support me, in any decision I made: it would remain a secret between me and her, she knew very well that Mom was against Nicola seeing or meeting us. I thought about it all night, although it wasn't a decision to ponder much: the very thought of seeing him already made me happy. The next morning, I told him that it was fine with me and that somehow, we would meet, even if in the presence of Eleonora. It was then that he had let it slip out: that for him there were no problems if she was there too, on the contrary! He would have liked to know her since he paid for her. I had fallen from the clouds. Some things often escaped my attention, but many others were deliberately omitted by my mother who, in doing so, was convinced she was sparing me further worries: this was one of them.

VII.

I TRIED NOT TO THINK TOO much about what would happen: when we were on the phone, for the sensations I felt it was as if he were there, always next to me; and yet I hadn't physically seen Nicola since the day we met him in Bari when I went for the first time to my mother's friend, the gynecologist. I planned everything with Eleonora: from the time to the location, from the apology to my mother to what Matteo and I would wear.

When the moment was about to come, I was restless all the night before; it was one of "those" nights when if I hadn't taken psychiatric drugs, I wouldn't have slept at all. In reality, I only managed to fall asleep when I took Matteo from his bed and put him to sleep next to me. His scent, his breath and the rhythmic beating of the little heart had relaxed me much more than those medicines that had poisoned me for most of my life, though still relatively short. And he, of course, liked the closeness even more than I did. Mom, who had never let me sleep in her bed, always told me I was wrong, that in that way I was spoiling him and that I would no longer be able to get rid of him even

when he grew up as if it were a compulsory or law-
ful thing, that of "getting rid" of one's children. I had
asked Eleonora, one day, after having argued about
this thing with my mother: is it really mandatory to
separate ourselves from our little ones like this? Why
can't we spoil them if we and they like it so much? She
replied that children are flowers and that, like flowers,
they must be watered and cared for, and that their stem
should never be cut cleanly from the rest of the stem
or the root. I had decided at that moment that, if I ever
had a daughter, I would call her Fiorella. I would have
pampered her for her whole life. And mine.

That morning was a splendid day, of unusual sunshine in the iron gray of Milan. We had arranged to
meet in the gardens of Via Palestro, at the benches
near the entrance to Piazza Cavour. I decided to dress
Matteo all in blue: it brought out the blond hair and
the blue of his eyes, the same as Nicola's; moreover, in
blue he would have seemed even bigger to his father,
who had seen him, though only from behind the windows of the nursery, for the first and only time on the
day he was born. Eleonora and I arrived early at the
gardens. I always hated being late, I wasn't going to do
it that very day. I wanted to enjoy his arrival from afar
and observe his reactions.

He was also dressed in blue; it was his favourite
colour. I recognized him immediately as he entered
the entrance and looked around for us. He was beautiful. The usual Ray-Bans worn over the eyes, long
straight hair and an unkempt beard. He looked thinner. He started smiling when he saw me. He raised

his sunglasses, revealing himself with his eyes to hook mine, and he did not distract them from my gaze. A forgotten feeling of well-being pervaded me. When he arrived in front of me, he reached out to caress my face: I acknowledged his gesture, leaning gently on his palm, and then I returned to get lost in his eyes. We continued to bask in each other's presence like this, without words or gestures that went beyond what we were feeling at that moment until I saw Eleonora arrive from behind him with the stroller. I broke the spell with delicacy, making a sign with my eyes. There was no need for anything else between us. He turned slowly and looked first at her then at the stroller. When Eleonora looked at me, I nodded to her with my head and she approached. She held out her hand to him, "Eleonora, pleased to meet you." He repaid her gesture out of politeness but in reality, he was only looking at that unforeseen son, too beautiful and so much like him: he released her hand and approached the stroller. Matteo looked at him, mesmerized by his long hair and mirrored glasses, and smiled at him, reaching out his little hands to grab both things at the same time. Nicola was waiting for nothing else: he looked at me to ask permission to hold him and I allowed it with a smile.

I could have died at that precise instant; I wouldn't have cared. Everything I wanted was there, in front of me. Nicola had been very sweet, but I had never had any doubts about it. He took him in his arms with such mastery that he seemed to have never done anything else before. Yet his legitimate children were already grown up. He placed him on his side, softly crouched in the crook of his arm, on the side of his heart. He sat down on the bench, under the plane tree that rained shade on him, so he could get a better look at him.: it seemed that the two were studying each other carefully. I averted my gaze from them to look at Eleonora who was crying. I caught her eyes: I silently asked her the reason for her tears and she replied by shrugging. When I went back to look at Matteo and Nicola, he too was crying and Matteo was stroking his beard. Just like I would have done at that same moment.

I let father and son get acquainted. I stood on the sidelines watching them flirt, one in the eyes of the other. When it was time for the feeding, Matteo protested, fumbling in the void of Nicola's arm in search of some milk. Nicola looked at me, undecided about what to do.

"I'm out of training," he told me, feeling sorry. I made a sign to Eleonora who busied herself with baby bottles and powdered milk since we had begun to incorporate it with my milk; I preferred to attach him to the breast in the evening, at the last feeding, and thus have the excuse of falling asleep with him. Eleonora took over Matteo again and sat on the bench in front of her looking for a warm ray of sunshine, while Nicola took me by the arm. We drifted away from them to find ourselves. As we walked, he wanted to know many things about how our lives had changed since we were in Milan and Matteo was born, if I would go back to studying and when I had an exam, what I was reading or writing, what I intended to do with my life. I did not answer this last question, but he reformulated it. I stopped and looked into his eyes, only then realizing how tall I had grown. Our eyes were almost aligned, whereas before I needed to look up to be able to look at him.

"Why do you ask?" I told him coldly, straight into his eyes. He held my gaze and caressed me: "In a couple of years, when the legislative term ends, I will not reapply ... I am old enough to retire as a senator ... if you want, you and Matteo, I will leave everything and we live together."

He sounded unconvinced as if he expected me to have excluded him a priori from a perspective of life together. When I smiled at him, he regained colour and breath.

"Are you sure of what you are saying?" I asked him before he could change his mind.

"Of course, I'm sure!" he said softly. "I haven't thought of anything else for a long time ... that's all! I just want to enjoy you ... no matter what happens or the scandal we would cause. Whatever happens, happens. I just want to be with you, if you want to be with me."

I threw myself on impulse into his arms and he welcomed me, fatherly and excited at the same time. It was then that Eleonora came upon us, with her stroller. "Your mother will be back soon," she said, making me feel like Cinderella of the fairy tale, who at midnight has to run away to avoid revealing the magical spell.

"I'm going back to Rome today, we'll talk tomorrow morning on the phone," he told me, then he went over to the stroller to look again at Matteo, who in the meantime had fallen asleep. He watched him enchanted to capture his changing expression.

"He is the only one who looks like me." He ran away crying.

That winter my mother had begun to feel unwell. I wasn't allowed to know what her ailments were, she hid almost everything from me. I think hers was a protective attitude towards me: she continued to consider me a child with too big problems for me to carry, not realizing how much I had matured both physically and emotionally in the meantime. When I pointed this out to her, she replied, "You will see, even when Matteo has grown up you will continue to protect him and to consider him little. It's normal when you are a mother!" thus truncating any further reply. Of course, I continued to have moments of impatience and crisis, especially when something interfered with the routine of my day, but I understood how it worked and tried to prevent them. This should have said a lot about my acquired maturity. But in her eyes, I continued to be little.

One day, returning from university, I found her at home when, on the other hand, she should have been at school. Eleonora, who had opened the door for me, indicated her room: "Your mother is not well." I looked at her curiously but she just shrugged: mom hadn't wanted to say anything to her either, but had made her call the doctor who followed her. He, after having visited her, had advised she should go to the hospital. Before leaving he wanted to talk to me and Eleonora, who was now one of the family.

"It's necessary to hospitalize her," he told us. "She had a fibroid. I told her that she should have surgery but she did not want to listen to me. Now I suspect that it has deteriorated and it is necessary to investigate." While he was talking, he looked at Eleonora in a strange way, and this did not escape me. When he was gone, we went into her room; she wept silently, slumped on her pillows. When she noticed us, she sniffed, to hide her tears: she reminded me of grandfather Giuseppe who pretended to cough when he felt like crying, so as not to show himself to others.

The next day, Eleonora accompanied her to the hospital. Mom hugged Matteo and me tightly as if she were sure she would never see us again, and I coldly shunned her: I didn't like these dull goodbyes in general, and that one seemed even more dopey than the others. She told me to count on Eleonora, both for me and for Matteo, because she would look after us until she returned. She could not imagine that, in reality, I counted much more on Nicola than on others. I couldn't tell her.

I stayed at home with Matteo. I was preparing the thesis; I had the defense presentation two months later. When Nicola phoned me, I told him the news about my mother. He was worried. Despite the natural aversion they both had, one towards the other, he was very sorry for my mother, who was the same age as him.

"Certain things shouldn't happen to mothers, so young, too!" he said, and he immediately placed himself at our disposal.

"It may be that it's nothing serious," I replied on the spot. But recovery was slow in coming. There was more than something wrong and the doctors were groping, doing analysis after analysis.

Nicola took the opportunity to get closer to Matteo and me. He showed up at the hospital and imposed his presence on mom. She, despite the powerlessness of fate, remained cold towards him: she had not asked him to stay close to me and Matteo but she had resumed to exact compensation, asking him to send me further financial help. For her, it was always just a question of money. She had always thought so, even in unsuspecting times, when we were still in Polignano and there were rumours of illnesses of someone she knew. Grandfather Giuseppe always said: "*Pov'r a ci capt!*" "miserable to whom it happens!" He explained to me that when you find out you have a bad disease if you don't have the money and knowledge to cure you, you won't survive. My mother said the same thing to Nicola in a faint voice, so as not to be heard by me. I returned with my thoughts to the day we arrived in Milan: I thought back to my dismay at seeing homeless people everywhere, abandoned in the cold and frost of their cardboard houses; I saw the taxi driver's hallucinatory gaze towards me when he replied, "The street is their home!" On closer inspection, his statement perhaps corresponded to reality, since it was thanks to Nicola and his money that in the end, we discovered how badly mom was suffering. She was transferred on the spot to the National Cancer Institute and began her *via Crucis*, which lasted just over two years. It lasted as long as two centuries, with darkness and light exactly opposite each other in an extremely harmonic dissonance that compensated the equilibriums. As with the stick and the carrot.

Grandfather Giuseppe often said "God gives and God takes away!" especially when he commented on news of this kind: in perfect ambivalence, he used this maxim of life for both negative and positive things. When I was younger, I did not understand the rationale for that categorical statement. If I asked him, "Then is God good and bad at the same time? Why does he give us something if he then takes it away from us?" He never answered directly. My question always fell into vagueness and his eyes wandered vaguely too. I got angry; I almost felt a grudge for that lack of attention towards me. Even a little girl deserves the explanations she asks for! And yet that grudge did not look good on me, like a dress three sizes too big, so I threw it away and dressed in elegant indifference, parsing time waiting for an answer that I knew would come.

God had given me Nicola but he had taken Polignano from me. God had given me Matteo but he was taking away my mother. My every joy was rewarded by the same amount of pain: was this perhaps the meaning of the unanswered questions from grandfather Giuseppe? How much other pain would I have to suffer to rejoice again? What other tests would I have to pass?

While mom was in the hospital, I graduated. Those footsteps trampled by time in Bari had re-emerged in Milan: it was easy for me to make up for the time spent giving birth to my son, "Studying is the thing you always do best," my mother told me when she was still fine. But she hadn't been able to come to my thesis defense presentation, she was too sick to leave the hospital. Eleonora and Nicola had come in her place. And Matteo, who had done nothing but clap his hands throughout the session.

While Mom was in the hospital, Nicola and his wife divorced. She said she was tired of his constant absences and decided to go back to New York. Yes, she was American just like Barbie! He had gladly accepted the news: after all, it was what he wanted. She had only anticipated the time, which Nicola had planned anyway to coincide with my coming of age. Their divorce had been very fast: mutual separation and consenting legislature had guaranteed their mutual freedom within less than a year, which was exceptional for those times. By mutual agreement, they had sold the Roman loft and the summer villa in Rosa Marina: with the proceeds of the sales they had bought a house for each of the two children with a lot of liquidity left over, which they had strictly divided in half. When she heard about it, mom made a "face": "Instead of thinking about Alina and Matteo!" she told him from her hospital bed. He, patiently, reassured her: "Nina, don't worry. Alina and Matteo will never have problems! Everyone knows what to do, *"si' accoime a faroine di sette setelle"*—"yes, like the flour from seven siftings."

I looked at him strangely, it was the first time I had heard him speak in Polignano dialect: "You speak like grandfather Giuseppe, but grandfather then explained what I did not understand," I told him almost annoyed because I had not understood the meaning of his answer that, in the end, was about me too. Mom replied: "In ancient times, to remove the bran from the flour, you had to pass it through seven increasingly thin sieves, from first to last. So, in the same way, when you have to speak: you have to think about it seven times in order not to make mistakes, in order not to offend anyone. True, Nicola?"

He nodded, amazed by Mom's response that, it was evident, had that bitter taste of apology, although unexpected.

He stored a few precious pieces of furniture from which he would never part, waiting to set up a house with me and Matteo, and he moved with us to Milan. In that house with the railing, which he had bought for us, there was room for five of us, comfortably: he had had some changes made by his trusted interior decorator who in a little while, in the space of a week, had made it even more beautiful than it already was. Mom had nothing to complain about, on the contrary: paradoxically she seemed relieved by his presence in her house, especially she who had been able to raise me by herself, without any need for reassuring male figures. Except for grandfather Giuseppe.

While mom was in the hospital, I enrolled again at the university, in the faculty of Psychology. I graduated eighteen months later, at the rate of one exam a month, including the thesis. Again, she hadn't been able to attend. She had been happy with pretending to look at the photos that Nicola had taken and that Matteo had given her too hastily to be truly looked at. She wouldn't see them anyway: she couldn't see anymore. During that year and a half, between entering and leaving the hospital, as if they were accounting papers of an existential budget, the cancer had rushed up her body, mowing her in a straight line from the uterus to the brain.

"We did not intervene promptly," his oncologist friend told Nicola as if to apologize to him for the ineffectiveness of the treatment.

VIII.

S HE WENT OUT ON A December morning, cold as
iron but swept by a wind so unusual that it had re-
moved all the greyness from the sky, leaving room
for the sun. I had left her asleep. I hadn't even said
goodbye to her, sure I would still find her there when
I returned. She hadn't eaten and slept for a few days.
She breathed with oxygen almost all the time but she
had always been quite lucid, so I was under the illusion
that in the end, everything would be resolved. That
she could last, though in that inhuman way, for a few
more years. Selfishly, that was enough for me. I gave
her a quick kiss. "I'm going to the University; I'll be
back soon!" I told her feeling confident, so I went out.
Via Verdi, via Bergamini, via Festa del Perdono: I went
there on foot, and in a quarter of an hour, I was already
there. I continued to tolerate subways and trams badly,
with the crowd of people always on top of me, at any
time of the day or week. All that noise which I "felt"
too annoying, stayed with me for days and days. I had
lost a lot of time at the office and when I arrived near
the corner of the house, I saw Nicola's car.

"How strange!" I said aloud, expecting him only in the early afternoon. I climbed even more lightly the stairs of the courtyard facing the house entrance, impatient to see him again, but as soon as I rang and they opened the door, the smile died on me. I understood immediately, there was no need to speak. He hugged me tightly but I remained cold, irrationally pissed at myself for not saying goodbye to mom properly, as if death were a programmable option with the remote control, postponed when needed. Unreasonably angry with her, who had chosen to leave just that morning while I was away.

I refused to see her. I preferred to be pissed off, imagining finding her alive later. I made my way to her desk, the one where she sat to do paperwork when she couldn't complete them in school. There was still her perfume, Chanel N° 5, unmistakable: I took the phone book and called Cetta; before Rosella, more for alphabetic rigour than for anything else. I was indiscriminately fond of one and the other. Cetta and Rosella had been with me and my mother when my grandparents died in Polignano. Now, despite the long silence and the separation that lasted almost three years, I knew they would rush to me in Milan. After all, Mom, in one of the last moments of her lucidity, made me promise to call them in Polignano, because she wanted to be buried there, in her home.

Cetta answered me immediately, on her first ring.

"What, she was next to the phone?" I had thought. "Cetta, I'm Alina," I said.

"Alina, baby, pass me Nina …"

"I can't, Cetta … Mom is gone."

A swift sob returned to me in response. "Who's with you, baby?" she asked me, not knowing the details of our Milanese life.

"Nicola, Eleonora and Matteo," I said quietly as if we had dined together the night before. Nicola approached me and motioned me to hand him the phone.

"I'll pass you Nicola."

"Nicola who?"

"I am Nicola Savino," I heard him reply.

I went to take heart in Matteo's arms, who had finished eating and still smelled of vegetable puree and Parmesan cheese. It was only a couple of hours after Cetta's phone call that Nicola told me: that day I also lost my father if you could define him that way. He was the victim of a car accident along with his second wife. Fate or chance, who knows: paradoxically, my parents had closed the circle of their lives together, as if my grandparents had planned that as well. "Who knows if they'll fight there too, wherever they've gone," I replied icily to Nicola. I hadn't shed a tear, but I turned off my eyes in mourning, silenced the radio from the things shouted and never said because the heart does not hear and the eye does not see. I felt like a dirty puddle, without depth.

Cetta and Rosella arrived the next morning. Both overwhelmed by grief, they first went to see mother at the mortuary of the funeral home that Nicola had called to manage all the funeral procedures: Milan was not Polignano, it was not allowed to keep the coffin at home with the dead inside, as had happened for my grandparents.

When they arrived home, I let myself be hugged tightly, there was so much nostalgia for everything that they both reminded me of. They were imbued with the smells of Polignano, even after a night spent on the train. Some scents seep into you but are released suddenly, triggered by who knows what factors; when you least expect it, they come out of Pandora's box to sow discord among the memories, to fight each other in the heart. My memories had gone to that afternoon of shopping for Marina's party in Bari; to the clothes tried on and then discarded, to the thousand excuses invented in order not to buy anything, even if in the end I had capitulated exhausted from fatigue; to the patience that Cetta and Rosella had had with Mom that afternoon. Because if they hadn't come, who knows, maybe we would still be there.

When Nicola came back with Matteo in her arms, they fell silent: they too were his old school friends as mom, and she, perhaps for that reason, despite trusting them, had kept them in the dark about who was the mysterious father of that child who had fallen out of nowhere nearly three years ago. They talked a bit among themselves while I, on the sidelines, made Matteo take his usual afternoon nap. Clarity had been made. Now it was necessary to move on.

Cetta and Rosella's suitcases miraculously gave out all kinds of good things, a sign that the traditions had remained so. We put on a "consolatory" table at a syn-chronized Polignano time zone and we continued to tell each other shreds of lives snatched from the rush of the day, between a plate of *orecchiette* and Murgia mushrooms, Coratine olives and Negramaro from Salento. Only tiredness prevailed over those scattered pieces of puzzles that we were painstakingly putting together. Nicola accompanied them to the hotel: the next morning would be the funeral, then we would go down to Polignano together. To close the chapter. Or maybe reopen it.

That night we slept together for the first time, I, Nicola and Matteo, finally reunited even in an official way. We almost felt like a real family. In reality, I hadn't been able to sleep who knows for how long: happy and sad, too much of everything in an emotionally unman-ageable reality.

Who knows, I thought, maybe this is the condi-tion of someone who has been really happy at least once in their life, but hasn't understood it; this swing between a sense of loss and a state of grace that per-haps will never be repeated or perhaps it will be as if being unhappy were a *conditio sine qua non* for having absolute proof of the existence of happiness. Because it, happiness, is almost psychopathic in its absolute ambivalence: a perfumed pearl hidden in the folds of dirty handkerchiefs inside drawers, a speck of gray dust in the corner, which passes a thousand times in front of us and you never see it, then that unexpected ray of sunshine appears, and you finally pick it up, even if to

throw it away. Comet-like visions of my life as I realized they were my present projected into the future.
Perhaps, in the end, that was true happiness.

I got up early that morning. Too many things on
my mind, a tangle of images and memories to pack,
not before having fulfilled the funeral commitment
in church: this already occupied three-quarter of the
space of my short-term memory. There would be a lot
of people, but certainly far fewer than there would have
been in Polignano if she had died there. Mum had
nonetheless been the principal of a large junior high
school in Milan, even though colleagues, teachers and
parents hadn't had time to really get to know her before
she fell ill. I still had a spoonful of low-fat white yogurt
between my tongue and palate when I heard Matteo's
laugh, beyond the chained doors of that house with
the wrought-iron railing. I hid like a thief behind the
door, but then I couldn't resist watching the two most
important pieces of my life playing there on the bed, as
soon as they woke up: I came out by surprise, mimick-
ing the lenses of a camera with my hands, to capture
the wide angle of that solar panorama that suddenly
emerged from the metallic nimbostratus.

Within the hour, we were all up. We would leave
Matteo at home with Eleonora, who was now like a
sister to me. She and Matteo would not come with
us to Polignano. There were four of us in the car, with
Cetta and Rosella, and we wouldn't have had room for
the two of them and my son's luggage. It was the first
time I was separating from him: I watched him having breakfast as if that were the last time I would have

seen him do it. I listened to myself saying the same things I heard from my grandfather Giuseppe when I had a snack with them in the afternoon: dip the biscuit slowly in the milk, otherwise, it will break; watch your finger when you pick up the cup; open the napkin, if you want to clean your mouth properly; you have long nails, we have to cut them, how is it they grow faster than mine? Now I understood many things: and grandfather, even though he was my grandfather, had remained younger than me. With the lurking fear of continuing to grow old, when he instead would have wanted me to remain small to be able to see me grow and never lose me.

"I don't understand time, what it is and what it is for!" I said aloud. Nicola turned, amused, to look at me. "What dilemma is affecting you today, baby?" he asked me. I shrugged. I returned with my thoughts to the suitcase and what I was going to take to Polignano.

The church of San Marco was our parish church. I had never been a regular visitor to it, but my mother, I think, went there every day, before going to school. It was on her way. The parish priest, Don Ambrogio, knew Mom and our history well and talked about it delicately in his homily. I listened to it casually, although it was short and concrete, like a true Milanese. Occasionally Nicola squeezed my hand to make me understand that perhaps it was appropriate for me to hint a smile at the priest's address. Distracted, I was too caught up in the architecture of the dome and the numbers on the sculptures: instead of listening to mass, I rattled off in my mind measurements, dates, styles and religious orders that followed one another over the centuries in that church. Cetta and Rosella, who sat next to me and Nicola at the first pew, next to the coffin, received the same condolences as we did: they were the only close relatives of my mother there in Milan, after us. Someone recognized Nicola and gave him condolences calling him "Senator Savino": I looked at him furtively, trying to understand if and how much it had bothered him but, even if it had been so, he did not show it. Outside there were quite a few photographers and journalists who had taken the opportunity to ask him a few questions. Cetta took the car keys from Nicola and, with Rosella, I went to hide there, to prevent them from taking pictures or questioning me too.

After the time to take the suitcases from the hotel where they were staying, we left immediately for Polignano. Nicola, more than used to these Italian road trips, between Rome and Milan, had also been missing from Puglia for some time: this was the first time we officially returned together. Cetta's husband, who was the deputy mayor of Polignano, booked us a room in a hotel: the grandparents' house had been closed since we left and our house had been sold when my parents had divorced, separating their belongings as much as their lives. Grandfather Giuseppe had had his say at the time: the house was registered in my mother's name, after all, he and grandmother Nenetta had bought it, so "That one doesn't deserve anything!" he told his daughter. But she, my mother, could not wait to close that too unfortunate parenthesis of her life and therefore, in order to get rid of that hindrance of a man, she had consensually accepted his request to divide the proceeds of the sale in half. Grandfather hadn't talked to mom for many days, but one of my banal influenzas was enough to bring them back together. Now they had finally reconciled. Even with my father.

Among the various things planned by the grandparents, at the time of their marriage, was a mammoth chapel in the cemetery, which should have brought together, in a few square meters developed mostly in height, both families. "United in life and in death" they had carved, in unsuspecting times, on the tombstone above the finely inlaid iron and copper door that closed that mausoleum. We would have buried them together, reuniting a couple who did not want to be reunited and separating one who, perhaps, would have liked to be reunited. But so it was decided and so it would be.

The burial of my parents was not the only task that awaited me: Rosella's husband, historical notary of Polignano, had already announced the opening of my grandmother Nenetta's will, scheduled for my eighteen years, which I would turn in a few days. We couldn't stop there until then: Matteo was in Milan with Eleonora and Christmas was just around the corner. Giovanni would have anticipated the opening of the will; grandmother Nenetta would have definitely approved. He communicated this news to us while we were stopped in an Autogrill, immediately after Bologna: he and Nicola, who knew each other well, had taken the opportunity to have a good chat on their cell phones, waiting to meet again in person.

We arrived in Polignano and we hadn't even noticed. Between a chat and another, a memory and
some news. We declined Cetta and Rosella's invitations to stop at their house for dinner. After having
accompanied them to their respective houses, we went
to the hotel to leave our suitcases and then to take a
stroll on foot, to stretch our legs and eat something.
Wherever we went, it was all about saying hello and
stopping to chat with the senator and offering condolences to Nina and Giacomo's much-talked-about
daughter. The rumour about Nicola and I had spread
quickly: two articles in the daily newspapers had been
enough. I was beginning to get tired of all that curiosity: I would have much preferred to be ignored, as
it had always been when I was little and went around
alone with my grandfather Giuseppe. Only then did
I realize how "famous" we were with our strange story
of love, subterfuge, escapes and a child out-of-mar-
riage between an over-fifty senator and a minor. I felt
like when mom took me to school. I was two years
old and she flaunted me as if I were a circus phe-
nomenon: as then, I was there with my mind greeting
perfect strangers but with my heart and nose up in
search of my lost steps in a past still too recent to be
forgotten.

    That night we slept alone for the first time to-
gether, Nicola and I. In Milan there was always Matteo
between us: with him in the middle it was a compe-
tition to see who gave him the most cuddles to make
him fall asleep and even when, exhausted, he finally
collapsed, we never felt free to enjoy ourselves in the

same explicit way as it had happened in our refuge in Polignano when our story began.

We returned there, in a strange circle that was struggling to close again, finally aware of the importance of our strange story and free from random feelings of guilt. What then, after all, is guilt? Symbolic transposition of rhetorical images? Absolute and binding truth? Grandfather Giuseppe always said, to console me when at school they unjustly accused me of something, that "The important thing is to have a clear conscience." Having a clear conscience is what it was all about: and mine was only right when I was with Nicola. I learned from his silences, from his looks, from his most infinitesimal gestures the simplicity of difficult things, the essential loyalty to oneself, because the first real symptom of a clear conscience starts from our integrity because if that is missing, everything is missing!

We made love like the first time. We were made of that same love: only amazement and sweetness, an outpost of wonder, with our hands exploring each other as if they were dashes, witnesses of the origin of a straight line but unable to draw its end; with the mouth distilling drops of well-being that departed from the soul and bounced in an expectation of sharing; with our dissonant but perfectly tuned souls on the same *solfeggio*.

"How is this alchemy possible? This unique perfection between us? This feeling of absolute well-being, what is it?" escaped from Nicola, between one lovemaking and another, and I did not understand if it was a question mark directed at me or if he was asking himself.

"It's just that it's you. And when it's you, I'm happy," I had replied half-sleeping some time later, with my hand caressing that small extraordinarily soft and hairless space between eyes and beard that accompanied me every night, in passing from wakefulness to sleep.

"Maybe it doesn't take much to be happy!" I told him in the car the next morning, looking out the window at that spectacular sea, with the waves smoking in the wind and the sky, blowing their noses on skimpy handkerchiefs of clouds, on our way to the cemetery. "Who knows why they have not understood it," I continued my monologue aloud, thinking of my parents who were waiting for us in the cemetery chapel, reunited again, still not by their will and perhaps forced now, beyond life, to that confrontation they had always denied themselves.

Nicola smiled at me as he maneuvered to park. "Not everyone is given our luck, but everything has a meaning in life! It is like when a parent tries to teach his children, and they never listen to him: those teachings are seeds that remain there, inside us, and then suddenly, after so many years, you realize that those seeds have become trees. What they didn't understand became our treed forest," he said. He always acknowledged my reflections.

IX.

"WHO KNOWS IF GRANDMA NENETTA and grandfather Giuseppe are watching us?" I asked him as I walked, hand in hand with him, down the same tree-lined avenue that I had travelled too many times with my grandfather. Same faces, same photos faded into memories, perhaps changed only in size, in perspective. Or maybe it was my perspective that changed over time.

The churchyard of the small cemetery chapel was crowded with so many people that not all of them fit inside. I shook Nicola's hand tighter and he reassured me. "Don't worry, I'm here," he said, while he was already starting to wave his hand to those he knew.

It seemed that half of Polignano was packed in ten square meters of courtyard: there were also Don Vito, whom I had not seen since my grandmother's funeral, and the mayor, with the tricolour sash across his chest fluttering spitefully around his face. Cetta and Rosella joined us before we even got to the edge of the crowd, they both hugged me.

"I'll be calm, don't worry," I said, but I wasn't convinced either. We struggled to enter the crowded church; inside were also dad's relatives. Cetta had led us along the very short aisle, in the middle of the crowded rows of pews. My father's relatives, friends and acquaintances were in the right-hand rows; we were assigned the left. Our pew in the first row. Everyone's eyes on us. I felt their breath, the sweat, the more or less obvious chatter and cheap gossip, the undisguised envy and the hatred towards me, as if I were the exe-cutioner and not the victim. I felt the vein on Nicola's hand throbbing hysterically. I traced its entire length and he turned to look at me, intrigued by the gesture.

"Don't worry about them," he said, approaching my ear just enough to make me breathe the silky smell of his beard. He knew me too well. He knew that his air was all that I needed to survive.

When the priest came in, they all fell silent. Not a breath, not a sigh, not a speck of dust, though copious, to rise from the ground. I tried to concentrate on the homily of that dried-up priest who recited mass from memory as if it were a litany, but I ended up wandering about the sparse altar, devoid of trappings and gilded furnishings, in stark contrast to the spectacular bronze chandelier; I stopped in the side aisle, full of tiny tombstones that contained nothing, only rusty letters, dates, name and military rank, the bare essentials for the families of those poor people who had fallen in war at any age. Finally, I lingered on that stranger's face.

I knew immediately who she was. She was just like him ... as elusive as that father we had unknowingly shared for some time. Who knows if she had made herself appreciated more than me, in the profession of a daughter, or if she too had disappointed him: certainly, as a female like me, she had interrupted that nominal chain, that game of handing oneself down in name to surname, which was so traditional. She was also not born a boy.

I escaped from the church dragging Nicola as soon as the priest gave us the blessing, leaving those curious faces in file to make condolences disconcerted. I needed to breathe clean air. He, having overcome the embarrassment and the human barrier that had been created, willingly followed me along the main avenue of the cemetery, then squeezed my hand tighter.

"We need to go to the mortuary, the priest has to bless the coffins," he said, but I didn't answer: I was with my grandfather Giuseppe, with my mind and heart, who told me all over again the stories hidden behind every tombstone or mausoleum I crossed, who explained to me the background of why there were no flowers on every grave since family quarrels had cut off for good what they should have strengthened. I was with grandfather Giuseppe, who projected me into the lives of others with that calmness that had always distinguished him, with lightness and attention to detail because, he said, "The details tell more than the whole story".

We reached the mortuary with the priest already inside. Outside, a lot of flowers, which could have embellished all the graves in the cemetery, and all the people we had left in the church, perhaps even a few more who in the meantime had joined the others to gossip. They made space to let us pass: they opened like the Red Sea in the book of Exodus and we crossed the sea walking on dry land. In the cramped room, cold with death and nauseating flowers, only a few people to greet the closed coffins. Cetta and Rosella with their husbands, Don Vito and the mayor, were with us and mom. With my father his wife, and his family. Even thinner than ours. I had finally looked into the face of that half-sister who looked like the spitting copy of my father.

"She looks like you!" Nicola told me quietly.

"And of course," Grandma Nenetta would have said, mischievously, "because females take after their fathers."

I thought I saw a smile directed at me when she realized I was looking at her, but her grandmother tugged at her and she didn't pull a breath: she recomposed herself in her fake pain, looking back into the void in the direction of the coffin. She seemed even smaller than her twelve years old, but I wasn't very reliable in that kind of evaluation. Who knows what I was like at her age: I had lost track of myself, in those dark years, I didn't even remember what I looked like; maybe I was like her, apart from "*u pagghizz russ*" that I inherited from my mother's family.

By the time we left, the flowers had been halved.

"The usual uncivilized," I heard someone say, "could they not at least have waited for the coffins to come out?" I looked in the direction of the voice and shrugged, knowing well the macabre tradition. "There were too many," I replied as the cemetery attendants hauled the coffins down. First mom, then dad, then the other. Nicola hugged me but I remained indifferent, as if I were not there, at my parents' funeral: I thought in the remote past tense as the only verbal tense to truly archive without forgetting, replaced, despite itself, by verbal tenses in the past that do not do justice to the stories, because between the two times there is a dividing line that does not real. A middle ground that speaks of what has happened and what has ended.

Hand in hand, Nicola and I had walked behind the cars on which they had loaded the three coffins. Behind us, a silent crowd followed, with a few lateral defections from time to time. Rosella and Cetta had filled their arms with flowers, which they placed left and right on the graves of their loved ones along the way.

"Take your time," the cemetery clerk said to Nicola, "because the workers still have to dismantle the stones."

He nodded, "It always ends up like this, you know what time you start but not when you finish."

It was then that I saw her in front of us, looking forlorn as she glanced at me sideways: she was hand in hand with her grandmother, who had dragged her along as if arriving first at the mausoleum was a guarantee of who knows what gratitude on earth, or from beyond.

"I don't even know her name," I said aloud about her with my eyes on her.

"Her name is Sara," Nicola said following my lost gaze, "diminutive of Serafina, the name of your father's mother."

I shrugged and stopped. "Wait," I said, and he looked at me worriedly.

"But what do you want to do?"

Someone heard our dialogue and even stopped to watch. I let go of his hand and approached her. I stopped in front of her, under the astonished gaze of the elderly lady who accompanied her.

"Hi, Sara," I said, extending my hand. "I'm Alina."

She, in turn, stretched out her hand, but then withdrew it. She threw herself into my arms. I too tightened her in my embrace, because similar people recognize and attract each other. I don't even know for what in particular, but it was a moment, like a vision of me, of my life. Like a vision of my present but in the past. Because at twelve you see the world from below and it seems disproportionate to your size: it's all too high or too low, too distant, too tiring. Her embrace was all that, it was melancholy, it was love denied, it was suffering and pain, it was a being not being, and only I could understand her. Share all that in an embrace.

The old woman then shouted at me: "She is mute, she cannot speak!" and then she yanked her, dragging her away from me with force. She protested, tried to free herself from that clumsy grip, gutturally shouted who knows what at that rude woman, but then she reluctantly capitulated, continuing to walk turned towards me, to look at me.

"But what have I ever done?" I said, continuing to look at the other me who was walking away. Nicola hugged me and I started to rain tears on his neck, breathing from him so as not to be suffocated by my crying.

Later I told him about me. Of my stolen childhood, of bullies, of anorexia and my intellectual and
sensory "superpowers", of my life before him, when I
was a fish out of water wherever I was. Wherever I went
or didn't go. I had always avoided the topic despite his
requests, but those accumulated tears had conveyed all
his questions, giving him those answers he had missed
until then. He listened to me like a child. He devoured
my first answers as if they were much-desired candies
and then when he realized he had almost finished the
package, he began to savour the taste so as not to finish them too fast. We took a nice walk hand in hand
through the tree-lined avenues and when we arrived at
the mausoleum the workers had already finished, there
was hardly anyone left. My gaze was captured by the
colours of the flowers mixed absolutely haphazardly
in the flower boxes, on grandfather Francesco`s and
grandmother Finella`s tombstones unlike those on the
tombs of my mother and her husband, pigeonholed
with floral expertise certainly by Cetta or Rosella. If
not both. My grandparents' tombstones were devoid
of any inscription to indicate when and how they had
died, no one having taken care of the task while we
were in Milan.

I had hoped so much to see myself again in Sara
that I was disappointed when I saw that only Cetta
and Rosella were waiting for us.

"Giovanni is expecting you at the study for the
will," Rosella said, and Nicola nodded.

"Aren't you coming together?"

They looked at each other in doubt as if they were not expecting an invitation. "If Alina wants …"

I replied by shrugging. "Of course, I want, you are my family!" But maybe I hadn't said it in the right tone: I was still thinking of Sara, I felt she was too much like me to abandon her like this, now that I had found her. As we walked silently towards the exit, I spit it out.

"What is Sara suffering from?" I asked quietly, "Why does she not speak?"

Cetta and Rosella looked at each other, almost accomplices. "Who knows, darling!" Rosella replied, and Cetta added: "They say that when she was little, she talked, then suddenly she stopped doing it."

I stopped suddenly, that last statement hurt my heart. As suddenly, I felt sorry for her mother too.

"Why does God give and then take away?" I said, again looking up at the sky, waiting for an answer from grandfather Giuseppe. But maybe he was with grandma Nenetta, playing Neapolitan cards for that last slice of *panettone* left over from Christmas as they did on those winter evenings because it was too cold to go out. Who knows how, however, that *panettone* was never finished. It was always there, even the following evening. And the one after that.

Grandmother Nenetta made her will the same day grandfather Giuseppe died. In a strange *consecutio temporum,* she had foreseen not only her death but also that of my mother, since she had left me everything she had, without even once naming her daughter Nina. I followed with unusual attention the reading by Giovanni, Rosella's husband, whom I had seen for the first time that morning in the mortuary since when I was little it had never happened. I wandered around long enough for a coffee, which the secretary prepared for us before starting "to break the ice," she said, not realizing that that cliché had no meaning for me. And while the others broke the ice with hot coffee in an all too evident obviousness, I thought of Dante's XXIV *Canto del Purgatorio*, of the "notary" poet par excellence, Jacopo da Lentini, who at a certain point in his life had put that sterile activity behind him to devote himself to poetry. I wandered with my eyes, lost in the ancient tomes under glass that I read behind him, in the elegant and tidy bookcase that covered the entire wall in front of us. There was also a very ancient version of the *Divine Comedy*, a sign that my comparison with the Dante notary was not so wrong. It was so beautiful that I got up to see it up close: I leaned my nose on it hoping to get drunk with its ancient scent of dusty oil, but the transparent barrier hadn't returned any stimulus to my sense of smell. Only Nicola's amused face and the astonished ones of Cetta and Rosella, beyond the clean glass.

Giovanni seemed very professional to me, even if it was the first testamentary reading I happened to attend. It was quick, also because I was the only heir: my grandmother had left me all the cultivated agricultural plots, some land suitable for building immediately close to the state road that connected Bari to Brindisi, two bank accounts (and for those he had given Nicola the written report), two houses in Bari and Monopoli and the house in Polignano. The house of my perpetual becoming. There were no other heirs. The will provided that the notary himself was my guardian, when my mother was also dead, unless in the meantime my health condition changed or other people able to protect me took over: in that case, on the spot, the notary in charge should formalize the successor to his / her role. He looked at Nicola as he read this passage, but Nicola did not move an eyelid. While I was signing for the acceptance of the inheritance, Giovanni looked at him again.

"Nicola, then? What are your intentions towards your son's mother?"

He looked into his eyes, seraphic.

"You are right: she is the mother of my son. For me, she doesn't need any guardians. She is perfectly capable of understanding, willing and managing her money as she sees fit! This does not mean that I will not always be by her side and that I will not give her all the advice she will need when she asks me for it."

Giovanni looked at me for assurance. Our looks bounced, even between Cetta, Rosella and me. Nicola was firm on his position. I looked him in the eye.

How many emotions never externalized, remain still in that lump in the throat! Because at a certain point in life you learn the subtle difference between holding a hand and chaining a soul.

"No, it is not true. I can't handle these things and you know it well. I need a guardian, someone to accompany me gradually in the things of life, and I want you. If you don't want to be my guardian, you will have to marry me!"

After a winter's silence, he started crying. "Alina, my love … I'm thirty-five years older than you!"

"So? What problems are there? Have there been any up to now?"

"No, you're right, but I didn't know you were so young, much more so than me!"

"We are still together, I don't intend to leave you … please, marry me!"

He remained steadfast in my resolute gaze.

"And don't cry, boys don't cry!"

They all laughed at my statement. "*Meh*! Come on! Please her!" Rosella said.

"After all, you have been together for a while, haven't you?" Cetta increased the dose. "Nico, then?" Giovanni asked him again.

Nicola got up. He went to the window, the one facing the sea. He was watching the waves, his arms folded. Then he began to speak as he turned his back on us, his gaze thrown into the blue of the sea. "I met her when Marina was eighteen. I loved her immediately. She looked older, not younger. She was much more than more. She was an 'everything'! I never thought of her as an adventure: she was just her! And I just couldn't help it. She is my everything, for sure I'll marry her!"

We got married in Milan in a civil ceremony, with Cetta and Rosella and their husbands as witnesses, the same day that our son became Matteo Teofilo Savino: every promise was a debt and Nicola had just paid his. And our honeymoon in Paris was fateful for us. The grass of the Jardin des Tuileries was enough for us to feel at home, with the scent of fresh meadows with early morning dew; the crisp and colourful air in the paintings of the artists in Montmartre; the suffused odour of fuel mixed with oil of the Bateaux Mouches along the Seine which, although stinky, smelled in my memories like the boats at Cala Ponte. It had been love at first sight. When Nicola said, jokingly, "I would move to Paris, are you coming with me?" I had no doubts and I immediately answered yes. The next day we were looking for a house instead of playing tourists.

X.

THAT NIGHT I DREAMED OF grandfather
Giuseppe. It was summer, at Lama Monachile's
white pebble beach. I was little, I could have
been maybe five years old. Blissfully in the water, with
the one-piece swimsuit that I liked so much and my
curly hair so water-soaked it almost seemed smooth
as if stuck on me like a dress. Grandfather Giuseppe
stopped to look at me from a distance, he hadn't
wanted to undress. He was watching me with the oc-
topus-shaped bathrobe in his hand, ready to put it on
me if I got cold. He always did this, but it turned out
that he was forced to take off his shoes and roll up his
pants because I never wanted to get out of the water.
The waves of the sea, the hiss of the wind, the flocks of
birds playing with the salt water offshore: it was all so
vivid in the dream that I felt the itch of salt on me, the
salty odour of iodine in my lungs, that cold thrill that
accompanies the only splash of the sea on the body
hot from the sun. Then, all of a sudden, I felt my heart
beating so hard it made me dizzy. Because there are
sensations that insinuate themselves so tenaciously

that not even the most extreme defences can prevent their invisible trajectory, right to the core. I woke up with my heart in my throat, with my thin nightgown glued to me. Sweaty as if I had been actually in the water. I got up very slowly, otherwise, I would have woken Nicola who was sleeping quietly next to me.

"You and your weird dreams!" he would say to me in vain, "but who says that something bad has to happen?" Yet he knew that when I have convictions, I hardly change my mind.

I left the room barefoot. I grabbed my robe and while putting it on I burst into Matteo's room. He too was sleeping peacefully; I saw a smile on him.

"That's good!" I said, my heart still distracting me with its hasty jumps. I went to the kitchen and took a look at the clock. It was early. I turned on the coffee maker and computer at the same time. A quick glance at the emails, between a spoonful of yogurt and the other, gave me three positive responses, all from the publishing house with which I was contracted: the approval of my last two editing jobs and the publication of my fifth book. Food for my frenzies. Writing and nothing else: it was cathartically therapeutic, whenever I would need other help in overcoming my difficult journey. Writing: I suppose I already possessed it, under my skin, but I didn't know it. How far had I gone, after my first novels were uncertain in style but written from the gut. My place in the world finally rediscovered, the essence of life itself.

As I sipped my coffee, my cell phone rang. "Strange!" I thought. The heart started bouncing back like a ping pong ball. On the display the number of Alessandro, Rosella's eldest son.

"What happened, Ale?" I asked him quickly, without even saying hello or good morning. My ear restored Rosella's voice.

"Alina, it's me, it's Rosella," she said in a rush. I breathed a sigh of relief but immediately thought of Cetta.

"Rosella! What happened? Is Cetta okay?" I asked her in syncopation, fearing an unwelcome response. When she said to me, "Don't worry, honey, Cetta is fine too. Sorry for the time, but I still have to give you some bad news. Sara's grandmother died," I immediately thought of the dream, of grandfather Giuseppe and of the funeral in Polignano. "Sara was entrusted to her, but now she is of age ... talk to Nicola, let's find a more dignified solution, otherwise ... I don't know how she can do it alone. Uncles or cousins don't want to have anything to do with her!" Rosella was telling me while I was fantasizing about her, about whom I had already written in my first book that I had published in Paris. I had already imagined everything and I had told the story, inventing from scratch something that was now coming about. Grandfather Giuseppe was right: God gives and God takes away. And vice versa.

I didn't need many words with Nicola. He immediately called Giovanni to understand how things were from a legal point of view. The judge had entrusted Sara temporarily to him and Rosella, as she had been declared unable to understand and know what she wanted.

"Can you imagine a little girl imprisoned in the body of a twenty-year-old?" he said to Nicola, "and she doesn't even speak, even though she has no physical problems that prevent her from doing so." Giovanni told us that he and Rosella had problems dealing with her: she was very stereotyped, full of fears and extremely selective with people. She slept very little and always ate the same things; when something changed in her routine, she went into a rage or holed up in the room they had set aside for her to draw. She drew everything, with any material that provided a suitable tip for leaving a mark, whether it was on paper, cardboard or wood.

"In short, in an untamed state," Rosella told me after. "In some ways, I feel like seeing you again as a child," she confessed. It was the confirmation I was waiting for.

It took a month to complete all the paperwork necessary: it was more difficult than we thought and Nicola had to bother many important friends, even at the Roman level when we still didn't know if Sara would have agreed to move in with us in Paris. And while Nicola worked in concert with Giovanni to obtain all the necessary certificates, I arranged to change the furnishings of the room we had decided to assign her, the one with a view of the Jardin du Luxemburg and direct access to the veranda. We called Jean Pierre, the architect who had renovated the house six years earlier when we moved permanently to Paris: we had become friends, indeed … it was thanks to him that I had finally found out what Matteo and I were suffering from. It was Jean Pierre himself who had told us about Asperger's syndrome. He noticed many character similarities between Matteo and his sister's son, who was affected by this very syndrome. He gave us the address of the neuropsychiatrist who had diagnosed his nephew, but in the meantime, I also studied the subject in depth. Strangely, it was a syndrome they had never attributed to me, among many others. I was sure that it was precisely the one I had suffered and still suffered, that Matteo had inherited from me and I in turn from my father. Too many coincidences, many similarities and fixations: the familiarity was evident. It's easy to talk in hindsight: when you know the substratum, you know how to fertilize the soil to make it fertile, even if that soil is stony.

Matteo was gifted with mathematics and technical calculations, which he put into practice with truly daring technical drawings and architectural projects. His artistic vein had become evident just as we were renovating the house: he had designed the furniture in his room, which looked like a ship in the middle of the sea at Polignano, and the furniture of the large veranda. There was a corner for each of us: I could write, he would draw and Nicola had his reading corner. Three distinct corners yet perfectly interconnected one into the other, just like we were. And a winter garden that he had designed in great detail so that I could use it as a vegetable garden and plant all those vegetables that were not available in Paris. His similarity with me had immediately emerged, in his behaviour, in his manic insights into topics that were difficult even for

older children; too many strange situations that, when
putting two and two together, frightened me. His difficulty in relating with peers was very evident: too many
mood swings and an underlying eccentricity made him
almost as naïve as I was as a girl. In the awareness of
the family equilibrium devastated by my special being,
I would not have wanted Matteo to be so similar to
me. But that was it.

When the neuropsychiatrist received us, she con-
firmed the diagnosis; in consideration of my past
experience, I was finally sure that this time it was the
correct one. Two specific tests were enough to deter-
mine that both Matteo and I were to be considered
on the autism spectrum. The autistic spectrum is *une
grande marmite*, a large pot, that contains a lot of ingredients to be cooked, she told us: there are "*enfants qu'ils
ne parlent pas, ils s'éloignent du monde totalment,*" that is,
there are children that are completely estranged from
the world; then there are "*enfants très intelligents, avec
un quotient de l'intellect très haut, mais ils ne réussissent
pas à communiquer avec les autres; ils sont hypersensibles,
hyperactifs, peut-être insupportables, maniaques, qu'ils
parlent beaucoup.*" There are very intelligent children
with a very high intelligent quotient, but unable to in-
teract with others; they are hypersensitive, hyperactive,
perhaps unbearable, maniacs and talkative.

When I had told her about my imperfect childhood, her eyes had lit up: they were naked, transparent
and thirsty for knowledge. She told us of the difficulties in diagnosing Asperger's in females, so I was a well
to explore, from which to draw miraculous water for

many other people who, like us, lived with the same syndrome. Because, while Asperger's males external- ize their problems, females learn not to point out their diversity, suffering in silence from their condition and merely observing others in order to imitate them. I suspected that Sara was autistic too: I planned on hav- ing her examined as soon as she came to us.

I went to get her in late spring. I went there alone, leaving Matteo, who was still going to school, at home with his father. Nicola was seriously skeptical about Sara's willingness to move with us to Paris: despite ev- erything, he had undertaken, together with Giovanni, the honours and burdens of all the files related to tu- toring power, with the possible reservation of officially taking over the adoption, if it was necessary due to her health condition. Giovanni and Rosella had told her everything, of course, but she had limited herself to nodding and signing the papers, without showing any interest or disinterest. They had also taken steps to put in storage the few valuable pieces of furniture of the house that they had put up for sale and had sent to our Parisian address a couple of suitcases containing the few personal effects they had recovered.

"She was very neglected, Alina. The grandmother was elderly but, may she rest in peace, she didn't really care for her granddaughter!" Rosella told me. "Since she has been with us she has almost been reborn and when I talk to her about you, her eyes almost light up. I am confident."

"I am too," I thought as I boarded the plane. The sky was completely clear of clouds, there was not a single small spot or streak of white or gray to splash the blue expanse. I smiled at the stewardess as I handed her my boarding pass and went to look for my seat, the one on the wing, near the window. I've always been terrified of airplanes and the first time I got on one was just when I came to Paris with Nicola. That time he had chosen the seat: he had told me that the spot was a "middle ground", not too far ahead to be sick at takeoff and not too far behind to suffer from landing, because "the most dangerous phases of an airplane trip are takeoff and landing; once you are up, you can rest assured!" Every one of his words was always pure gold.

I had brought my Walkman with headphones, with my beloved Smashing Pumpkins in my ears; I listened to them and listened to them again with my eyes closed at least three times, so long had the direct flight to Bari airport lasted, that I hardly noticed and I was already there. I looked out the window the moment I heard the wheels roll on land and I started breathing again, with my heart back in place and no longer sauntering in my throat. Getting off the plane ladder further reconciled me with myself and with the whole world. A breath of sea air opened the door to my dormant memories. I had become a child again. When I went out into the hall I greeted Alessandro, Rosella's son, who had come to pick me up. In the car I asked him to tell me about Sara and about myself, about when we were little, for those few times we had seen each other. I was not of much company then. And I still wasn't. He told me that Sara too was a solitary type. She preferred to be alone, though looking out the window. She drew everything she saw. "She has been drawing smiling female figures with red hair for two days," he said, pointing to my hair. "I think she will be very happy to see you!"

She had heartened me, more than the home air had already done. I was sure that Sara would finally have closed the circle of my life, completing its perfection. That sister ... maybe she was the Fiorella I had dreamed of, that much-desired daughter that I hadn't had.

It was so hot it felt like summer, even though spring had just begun. Alessandro accompanied me to Rosella's house. She and Sara had gone for a walk by the sea, so Giovanni told us when we went up to leave the suitcase.

"Here we are ready to eat, you go and retrieve them *abbascie a lu purt*," he had told me to look for them at the beach in Lama Monachile. I had reached them. They were there, right in Lama Monachile, as in the dream of that night, when upon awakening I learned about Sara's grandmother: Rosella was reading a book, sitting on a beach chair on the shoreline; Sara instead was sitting on a towel, looking at the sea and then drawing. They hadn't noticed me. Rosella was reading aloud: when I approached and she noticed me, she fell silent. She put her hand to her mouth, as she had always done when she wanted to show amazement and contentment; as she had done in Milan when she had seen me again after so many years. Sara hadn't noticed anything, perhaps not even Rosella's silence, at least that was how it seemed to me.

It was not so. When I came in front of her, she looked at me and then resumed drawing me. She had touched up the red of the hair on her drawing, slightly darkening its contours and lightening the reflections of the sun with gold. She studied me again as a lurking feline, starving with that hunger that devours everything, that atavistic thirst that is already there to consume you, that fire that burns everything. When the drawing was finished, she got up, she touched me with her closed eyes and her heavy breathing, then her words took shape like magic. Her voice had cuddled me slowly as she hugged me, like a caress on the heart to fill the missing voids inside. "Alina." Only this she said to me.

We hugged each other tightly under Rosella's watery eyes, even more so than the sea.

"I won't leave you anymore! I won't leave you anymore! " I cried in the crook of her neck; she had become as tall as me, and when we looked at each other, beyond the tears that rained down, we were mirrored in each other. We were the same, exactly complementary. She my blonde version. Me the red version of her: two half people finally completed. And Rosella, on the other side of the mirror, with that happiness on her so great that, if looking at her carefully, when you retell the moment, you can only say: "I was so happy that I would have died with a smile!"

Even the clouds run without counting minutes. It was raining behind the window the morning we arrived in Paris. It was one rustling, plush rain, of those that reveal something only by murmuring, as it slides on the glass to gather in the eaves.

"Similar people attract each other," Nicola assured me on the phone, while the streets of Paris chased each other behind the windows of the taxi that took us home from the airport. Her hand in mine, Sara hadn't let go of me for a minute during the whole trip. On the plane, her grip had been strong, attentive to the same deafening noises and air pockets that from time to time annoyed me during the trip: I tried to make her listen to my music, but she refused to wear headphones, preferring the earphones from one of the hostesses. Even at the airport, in Paris, she had shown some difficulty in adapting that she had not manifested in Bari, but the Charles de Gaulle was too big a seaport even for me, who knew it by heart. Only in the taxi had she let go slightly, attracted by the frantic speeding of the cars along the immense avenues, with her nose stuck to the window wet with raindrops that began to fall.

When we crossed the threshold of the house, she glared at Matteo and clung even more tightly to me. In fact, I wasn't sure she was really looking at him: more than anything else she gasped in the void, breathing at the same rhythm as my heart, on which her ear had rested. He avoided her gaze, searching his father's eyes for confirmation that we had arrived on time. Then she released my embrace and Matteo embraced me as if I had come back from who knows what distant continent. She started wandering around the house: together we followed her as she looked into every room, opening doors without fear of the unknown, until she reached the door of her room, on which Nicola had hung a wooden structure, in contrast with the pure white, with the name Sara written on it. Only then did I realize that each door had been equally decorated with our names. It was not the only change made to the house in those three days: he and Jean Pierre and his team had worked miracles. Sara and Matteo bonded immediately. The time to sniff each other like dogs, to mark their own territory, and they were in each other's arms.

XI.

WITH SARA, IT HAD ALL been a crescendo. Like when, as a child, one is weaned from the mother's breast and begins to spit out baby food and smoothies, before realizing that they are good; when one starts throwing up little words at first incomprehensible and then gradually more and more structured until one never stops doing it; when one crawls and falls and gets up, before learning to walk on his own legs, and then to run and never stop. So, it had been with her. With my Fiorella.

The diagnosis of our neuropsychiatrist was more than obvious. She was very exhaustive, in consideration of the fact that Sara's autism was of a different form than the one we were suffering from. She was low-functioning autistic, with manifestations of the syndrome much more evident than ours. The very reduced verbal functions and the evasion of glances were too important evidence and only partially recoverable: of course, if she had been helped from an early age she would not have been at this point. Certainly, she would never be completely cured: I had learned that autism is not a disease, and above all, it is not a disease that goes away, even if treated with the right medication. Autism is a way of being and existing, detached from the common rules of behaviour; it is widespread hypersensitivity, evident hyperactivity; it is looking "beyond" something that cannot be found elsewhere. I had proven on my skin that autism is like the sea, it is a state of mind: you can be miles away from it, but you always carry it with you; it is life and destruction together; it is that moment of apparent calm that makes you make peace with the world while the northwest wind, the mistral, is rising. That sea in flow that at night drags all the terrestrial dirt off to return to us in the morning in a calm state, with sleek stones, smoothed by salt and scented with iodine and algae.

Matteo and Sara had grown up like this, on our happy island, both strongly opposites of each other. If they had been one person, they would have naturally compensated themselves but, separated, they were a true force of nature. Matteo, apparently able-bodied from a physical point of view, was certainly intellectually and culturally hyper-gifted, much older for his age, albeit immature from a relational point of view. Sara, also apparently able-bodied, but with ingeniously childish attitudes and still too lazy to be able to pronounce a few words that were beyond those strictly related to her very survival. Their life flowed on different tracks, visible only to expert eyes and accustomed to their perfect imperfections.

We hired two educators for Sara so that she could recover all that she had lost until then—the unconscious victim of ignorance and cowardice. She initially refused any help that did not come to her directly from me. With infinite patience I always remained close to her, supporting the educators. Nicola looked at us amused, from afar. He didn't like some of the methods used, but he changed his mind when we started getting the first answers from Sara, albeit contained, to our questions. Of course, it cannot be said that she had become completely self-sufficient, but already washing and dressing alone, eating, reading aloud to hear her voice again and writing, where before she only drew, were unexpected achievements that, instead, she had obtained.

I wrote a couple of books about our history: I wanted to be of help to all those families who had read about fatigue, hopes, disappointments and unexpected victories; I wanted to be of active support for those families who did not have sufficient financial resources to allow all the therapies to which we subjected Sara and Matteo every day.

That same God who gave and took away, at least from an economic point of view, had been magnanimous with us: between Nicola's senatorial annuity and the royalties from the sale of my books, now published all over the world, thanks to God, we had no financial problems.

What worried me instead was the state of Nicola's health, who was beginning to be of significant age. That wicked age that always makes you feel young in spirit but then leaves you physically on the ground. He was weighed down by the objective difficulties that began to affect his life, no longer allowing him to do everything he had done up to then. He had been complaining for a couple of years when we made love. He always said: "Bastard old age! We no longer make love; we make affection!" I joked about it, aware that our age difference, from a physically conjugal point of view, only became evident then, after almost thirty years of fulfilling life together. I did not give weight to these utterances. That had never been my priority with him. Then I tried not to let this nonsense weigh on him, even if in my heart I became impatient when I found myself in difficulty; when I could have done things faster alone, but he was there and I had to respect his rhythms. The essential thing, however, was to have him next to me.

We continued to take hand-in-hand walks along the Seine; we stopped to chat in the company of the Italian street artists we passed; we lingered in the *passages de Paris*, the covered Paris galleries when it rained. In short, we tried to do what we had always done, but I was beginning to notice his real fatigue. I perceived it from the tremor of the hand, from the "false" stops to look at shop windows, obligatory stops to catch his breath. He never lost his style: he still wore an unkempt beard, only whiter than before, and his hair was still long, only grayer. We had spent a lifetime together, but I still didn't get tired of him. I was still jealous of him and the looks he attracted.

When they called me from the Municipality of Polignano for the sale of some land, the last remaining of grandmother Nenetta's inheritance, I had no doubts: I would have brought Matteo and Sara with me, but not Nicola. He would stay home in Paris. Too heavy, the journey. The building's doorman, Philippe, and his wife were more than trustworthy people, we had known them since we bought the house, over thirty years earlier: they would look after him until our return. But he waited to know we were physically distant to spare us the pain of separation. He let himself die alone in the afternoon, with a smile on his face and perhaps our thoughts with him.

That day had been heavy for us in Polignano. We started work on the house with twelve rooms because Matteo fell in love with it and was adamant: we would go back to live in Italy, there in Polignano. In no time at all, he presented his project to the Municipality, after having worked on it for a whole night at Antonio's studio, Rosella's son, who was a surveyor. That day they had dismantled and reassembled all the "chianche", the limestone floor slabs, typical of the rural buildings of the Apulian territory and of *trullo* constructions, after having redone the pipes below: We had been up from five in the morning, but the satisfaction was as obvious as the tiredness. The day had flown by, but it was nothing new: Matteo was used to these *tour de force* when he worked, even if he continued to marvel at the goodwill of the Italian workers who, compared to their French colleagues, no matter what they said, were much faster and more accurate. Even cheaper and used to long hours of work. In France, it was not exactly like that.

"Shall we go eat? *J'ai trés faim!* Alinaaaaaaa!" Matteo shouted, distracting me from my thoughts.

Looking at Nicola's now vintage Rolex on his wrist, "You're right, it would be time!" I answered while I was collecting Sara and our things in no particular order. "Have all the workers left?" I asked him, but he did not answer, because he was already outside the door, headed for the same place, which we had discovered the first evening we ate there, as soon as we arrived from Paris, along the old walls of Polignano. We immediately felt at ease, in that atmosphere between the rustic and the sea that was so congenial to us. We got in tune with the owner of the place: he was a nice guy, always smiling and carefree. The next evening, when we returned there, his father, who had been a pupil of my mother, was there and he immediately remembered me. He recognized me by the hair which, according to him, was an unmistakable red. I didn't believe him for a moment. Rumors circulate fast in small towns.

That evening he observed Matteo with curiosity, with the suspended gaze of someone who knows but wants confirmation. When I introduced him to him, he said amused: "I thought he was your husband!" Matteo laughed at us and replied: "*Mon Dieu*, never!" We entered into familiarity with him and he, who was helping his son in the dining room, took the courtesy of always reserving the same table for us, in a secluded corner of the room. Big enough for eight, it was our work table, as well as a table full of appetizing local pickles.

Cetta and Rosella had obviously competed to have us with them. Conventional southern hospitality with them took on far wider meanings. In order not to upset either of them, I was inflexible: we would sleep in a bed and breakfast and eat aimlessly, as Matteo and I were accustomed to, for the whole week, otherwise, we would not have concluded anything on the construction site. On Sunday, however, they could take turns inviting us to lunch.

I had told Matteo a thousand times about Sunday lunches at the grandparents when I was little: the magic of memories or my way of telling him had fueled his imagination, so much so that he had grown up with the myth of grandma Nenetta's ragù, cooked in the large heavy aluminum pan, with bay leaves and pork belly in the meat rolls. In Milan I had never managed to find the same cut of meat they used here, the meat did not "melt" like my grandmother's. In Paris, least of all, even if I had learned to cook other things: Nicola had always been very demanding of me. I was already used to excelling myself, so every day was for us continuous experimentation, discovering the mixed flavours that tasted of sea, land and sky together. The sea of Polignano, the Po valley land and the French sky, with its game: as a *trait d'union*, all the possible and imaginable spices that I had learned to grow, in my Milanese courtyard before, in my winter garden in Paris then, and which I now had in mind to repeat here too. But I did the math without the host, the host who has our destiny in his hand and enjoys mixing the ingredients, mocking our orders and upsetting our menu, with all those neat and tidy and only imagined delights.

"The order has been taken," I said to Matteo as he came from the bathroom and approached our table.

"Then I'll take this opportunity to call home! Have you heard from dad?" he asked me, taking the phone from the jacket hanging on the chair.

"Yes, I heard from him before. Tell him I'll call him later, before I go to asleep." I looked around distractedly for familiar faces, friends in blurred memories or a new generation of strangers, but it didn't seem like there was anyone worthy of my attention. The project to be reviewed is more interesting, I thought. And as I looked at the drawings, trying to figure out if and where we were late, I heard a strange silence. I looked up in a latent unreality and watched Matteo whiten. He looked like a rag on the phone.

"Dad … he's gone!" He barely had time to tell me this before running to the bathroom to throw up. Sara started screaming and my blood was running cold.

"No, it's not possible, not him," I said to myself, trying to chase away that cloud that had enveloped us in a funereal chill. I hugged Sara, containing her pain on my heart, but the evening was pitch-black. I couldn't show anything, least of all the boulder that was oppressing my heart and stomach. I suffocated the urge to retch because I would have cried bile.

I made frantic phone calls to Cetta and Rosella. I left Sara at Rosella's while Alessandro accompanied Matteo and me to the airport. The distress had taken over her, in the car. We bought the last two seats on the first plane to leave for Paris, although we would make a stopover in Beauvais, 90 kilometers away, instead of the usual Charles de Gaulle. Check-in, also on the fly, hadn't even given me the time to realize

that I was getting on a plane without my usual rituals.
I hadn't even noticed that I was sitting and with the
safety belt on. I closed my eyes, pushed away thoughts
and pain, flew over Italy and France almost without
realizing it.

Philippe and his wife had found him in his study,
slumped in his favourite armchair with still a faint
breath of life; they immediately called the ambulance,
but he was dead even before exiting the front door.
They had taken him to Saint Vincent de Paul anyway.
They were still there with him. The pain had crept into
the flesh, right under the last layers of skin, where un-
derneath there is nothing but blood and soul.

We hired a car at the airport, to get to Paris as
soon as possible. I told Matteo that I would drive the
car: too much mud in his eyes. In mine, I do not know
what there was, perhaps only a devastated and thun-
derous nothing. Matteo was a dead weight. I took him
by the hand and dragged him out of the garage where
we had parked the car. When we entered the large hall
of the hospital and asked for Nicola, we were directed
to a doctor not far away who was talking to another
couple of desperate people like us. Who knows whom
they had lost. He himself approached us: he explained
what had happened and why they hadn't been able to
revive him, then he called a volunteer to accompany us
down to the morgues. He squeezed our hands tightly
without offering condolences, saying only "*Bonne
chance!*". Matteo did not want to come in to say goodbye to his father with me. I left him with Philippe and
his wife, more destroyed than us.

I was left alone in that cold and anonymous room, crying all my tears, all the ones I had kept at bay until then. I remained in that icy place of blood and flesh with their rancid stench, cold and trembling with rage. Tired. Betrayed. Empty. I watched him smile in his inert pose, for he seemed only asleep. How many times had I observed him like this, awake in the night, infinitely thanking whoever had granted me his life next to me: too many times I had slept, clinging to his body, caressingly close breathing his beard. That same beard remained silky even without life, the essence of life itself.

When I went out, Matteo was there, left shapeless on the rigid iron chair like a cloth, left to dry in the air after you washed the dishes. I didn't need to tell him anything. The exchange of glances said everything. It would be days, months, years. Instants. The pain would remain, lurking like a hungry dog. We would have let the air flow freely because grasping it would no longer be possible, without him it would not have returned its vital oxygen. We thought of the same life at the same time: Polignano and Sara. We would leave again to be with them.

XII.

THE NEXT MORNING, ALTHOUGH TORN by pain, I went home alone. Matteo found it too agonizing to go to an empty home, entrenched himself with his pain in the suite of the hotel where we were staying, leaving only to perform the physiological functions of vital nourishment, what was necessary to give him strength and desire to move forward. Out of breath, despite not having made the stairs on foot, I arrived at the door of that house that had hosted us for almost thirty years. That same house that smelled of redemption, of rediscovered joy, of awareness and love. Of Nicola. His presence-absence was overwhelming. The warmth of disorder. All over, everything was still, like when you exit the house too quickly, having to return shortly thereafter, and leave all the windows open, the clothes hanging on the balcony, the glass on the table with the book open on the last page read. The scent of him was still on the armchair where he had died. His favourite corner, between sofas and bookcases and too tidy end-tables, as he liked.

I would have liked so much to have been able to clear away the heavy memories and return to make room for my intellect, which is not easy when anxiety oppresses you and digs into a void as big as an abyss. Written and unspoken words were the only way to stay poised on the edge of the precipice, so as not to fall into it. They crowded my mind, in a confused muta- tion of images, sounds, smells, colours. They smelled of wind, sea and river, of sand and mud, of rain. They knew of distant times, at least three lifetimes ago. They knew of poetry fading in the shadow of other words that pushed in a race to look out the window. Only handfuls of letters to hide the power of infinite pos- sible shades of meanings. It is easier to write when pain gnaws at your soul. Apparently, an oxymoron, to talk about love when you no longer have love in your heart. Him, only him. Only the memory of him could comfort me, quench that insane thirst for hatred and revenge that was wearing out my soul. Why? Why? What had I done wrong in my life, to accrue all these punishments?

I wrote over five thousand words in one go, so many were the ones that the counter at the bottom left of the screen displayed for me. They had not been peaceful years, far from it. I could have written so many books about it, to tell my story. With photos ripped and then reattached. Polignano, Milan, Paris and then Polignano again and now Paris. Close the circle with Matteo, my reason for living. Pieces of puzzles to reas- semble, after mixing the tiles that give off the odor of salt, with the colour of the winter rocks in Polignano, when we went there secretly to see them frolicking with the waves, a bit like us; they taste of metal and smog, with the livid gray of the fog that fades into intense blue, when the sun peeks out on fine days, in Milan; they taste like honeyed sugar in pastel colours and the consumed petroleum of the *Bateaux Mouches* along the Seine, in Paris. Because everything has its own time. The important thing is to flow from one to the other, in a solution of continuity that does not admit regrets.

While I was ideally closing those open windows on the balcony of my life, I photographed the moments, as if they were frames to be reread in sequence. I saved them on the pen drive: they would have been the ideal beginning for my immortal love story. In the end, I let my gaze wander around the salon in search of something that would take me back in time, that would give me back his smile and blue eyes, his now white beard and long hair, still as when I had known him. I filled a few suitcases for me, Matteo and Sara. Not like Mom had done when we ran away from Polignano. She had preferred to leave behind open doors to close, but she hadn't had the time and the will to do so. While I was waiting for the taxi that would take me back to the hotel, I called Philippe, down at the reception, and asked him to come up to me. I had taken out of the fridge the things that were about to expire, I had filled a couple of bags to leave him, along with the keys and the bills to pay: he and his wife would have enough to eat for at least a week, as we did back home, after funerals. I gave him precise instructions. He would follow the removal of some furniture that I wanted to relocate to Polignano and some books, which I had particularly singled out for myself: there were some really rare and expensive ones, the result of years of research shared with Nicola; they would always be close to me, earthlier than him. His wife would follow the selection of my clothes, that of Matteo and Sara that I was leaving there: they were tasks that I would have preferred to do myself, as when you change your wardrobe from one season to another, when you take the opportunity to throw away a lot of stuff or find so much more, set aside and then brought out again for the occasion, but it would take me much more time than I had. We stayed in Paris for the time strictly necessary to manage the funeral and to close the house.

After all, I was leaving behind "only" thirty years of life history lived frantically: I had never really considered the years lived in Milan, as mine, even though it was there that Matteo was born and there that later I married Nicola; the French parenthesis and Sara's arrival had been much more important to me. Because you feel immediately those who make you feel good, like the smell of coffee before drinking it or the scent of bread before biting into it. And I was transformed with them at my side. From the rough paper I was before, I had turned into soft cotton.

We returned with Matteo's Jeep. We brought the rented car back to the airport and drove straight to our destination, non-stop from Beauvais to Polignano in only seventeen hours and four obligatory stops. We talked very little on the way: mostly about the housework and the finishings, the road and the weather, the traffic and the people we crossed in passing at the gas stations. About white snow from afar, first on the Alps and then on the Gigante glacier; of the different colours of trees and meadows, of the change of territory from France to Italy. When the sun set, we fell silent, lost in our thoughts, mesmerized by the street lights and the rain we had passed. It rained on the road but, at times, also from our eyes. We arrived in Polignano late at night, but Sara was still up waiting for us. She welcomed us in a hug that was worth more than all her unspoken words.

When I woke up the next morning, Matteo had already gone out. I left Sara at Cetta's and went to our castle. They, the workers, were all so busy that they almost didn't notice my presence. I went up to my childhood room. And I was lost.

"Alinaaaaaaaa! Alinaaaaaaaaaaaa!" Matteo's voice bounced from room to room. I listened to it from afar as if it did not concern me, lost in the same majesty that I had left behind the day after Grandma Nenetta's funeral. He was already there then. He was more than an embryo in my womb. We were alone, me, him and the sea. I told everything only to the sea. In truth to my grandmother too, but she was already on the verge of death and she had not answered me. She seemed tired, very tired. I had left her to rest but she had never woken up again, overwhelmed by the pain of memories. Or perhaps from the manifestations of that too strange granddaughter that insisted on giving her concern. That don't-know-what masochistic thing about love, when you think you don't deserve it. I had come to hole up right here, then, to escape the anonymous faces saying the same empty words, with unwelcome hugs soaked in garlic and sweat. Silly funeral rites that englobed my boredom even more and delayed the already unwillingness to share something that, shortly thereafter, would be more than evident. I remembered Rosella who ran around with mom in search of grandmother's last good dress, in that wardrobe that was always too fragrant with talcum powder, lavender and mothballs; Cetta making coffee with grandpa's big coffee-maker, with her noisy echo spreading from the chimney to here. The scent of cinnamon and sugar, in the air, mixed with the unmistakable smell of the winter sea. I could still feel it, even if we weren't in winter, an indelible imprint in my heart.

I looked out into the dusty corridor full of footprints that trampled each other.

"Follow Tom Thumb's crumbs, mine are the smallest ones!" I answered him to make him understand where I was. He appeared at the door of the room, two doors away, and I returned there. I heard his hasty footsteps; he was eager to update me. He yelled at me when he entered, feigning a false astonishment with his hands firmly anchored to his hips, in an attitude of obvious disapproval.

"Already! I should have imagined it!" I turned around laughing to look at him: it was the same story every time. "You are a bad actor! What's up?" I asked him, returning to dive with broken eyes, hearts and memories into the mirror of the window overlooking the sea.

"They've cleared out the cellar, do you want to come and see it?" he said to me, looking at me with an amused face waiting for my obvious answer.

"Do I really have to?"

I set off spontaneously. My footsteps in his. He was just like his father: every time I thought about it, the pain bit into me, like raging dogs. He came back to check the work in each room and I followed him. In one, the fixtures were missing, in the other the parquet or the baseboard or the painting and the electrical system. There were at least three busy workers working, for each of the rooms on the floor. The made-to-measure furnishings were almost ready. As I walked, I glanced at the dry walls of corridors and stairs, they were just as I wanted them to be. And while I was already imagining everything, I heard Matteo yell at one of the masons: "You are an idiot! Fuck, Tonio! Here the joints were not supposed to be closed! *Ciaparat*, bug off!" Their bickering was ridiculous, with Tonio speaking in strict Polignanese and Matteo in his particular pseudo-Milanese, which somehow, he had never lost, sharply mixed with Parisian. I did not know how they understood each other. I went, amused, straight to the cellar, which was no longer a cellar. The old door replaced by another armoured door, custom designed. It was already there even before I went upstairs to lose myself completely, but it was sealed with cellophane. I looked at it but did not see it.

I remained stunned in front of it, amazed even more than I imagined. I breathed a strong sigh before opening it, in an obvious gesture of eternal memory, when you know you are doing something for the first time that you will never forget. I descended the narrow staircase that unfortunately remained so due to architectural constraints, and when I got down, I was out of breath. I closed my eyes already blinded by the dark, restarted the images in my mind, in search of the same strong smells I had left more than a lifetime ago, but nothing would come back to me except blurry photos that smelled of aged wine and cheeses and fresh sausage hanging to dry. I slowly opened my sore eyes and they hypnotically moved towards that only certain source of light that emerged, though dimmed by sunset, from the large reinforced glass oval window that we had dug inside the mighty wall, close to the sea. The engineer of the municipality's technical department was the son of an old friend of my mother's. He had turned a blind eye, maybe both.

The smell of age-treated parquet treated was strong; the latter covered the rise created on the old concrete floor to isolate the room from the neglect of humidity, which was also under control thanks to the dehumidification system installed, which arrived in record time from Finland. I imagined everything blindly: cleaning done, systems turned on, books in their place, sheltered beyond the glass windows, comfortable armchairs and soft lamps. In the silence of the darkness, I heard Matteo's footsteps coming down the stairs. I turned to look at him.

"Resolved with Tonio?" I asked him. Instead of answering me, he suddenly turned on the lights, making me jump so much that I closed my eyes again. I smiled at them even before opening them again.

"So, you like it!" he said sure of himself, looking at me over my shoulder. I didn't need to answer him, my sign of agreement was more than exhaustive. "I can't wait for it to be all over!" I told him then, taking his hand too big next to mine. He let it be squeezed and I relaxed. With my imagination, I was already here, in my refuge, a place of study and flights of fancy. I would write my books here. With the sea next to me and the scent of memories on me.

Matteo had also thought of Sara. Her artistic streak demanded light. She, who played with colours as if they were words, liked to paint pictures and decorate fabrics: he assigned the remaining wing of the first floor, with the studio overlooking the atrium with the skylight, to take the light to paint from high, while the bedroom had a window on Piazza dell'Orologio, to be able to watch the walkers-by and capture in a photographic imprint all those faces that she still only looked at from afar, only from afar. The second floor became a bed and breakfast with access from the external staircase at the rear. Luxuriantly flowered and accompanied, on the unreachable top, by ancient scissors, all rusty, which I had recovered from an antique shop on Quai d'Orsai, when Nicola was still there. I had wanted them badly, so much so that when I had explained to the shopkeeper the meaning that we Polignanesi attributed to them, he had given them to us. "*Alors, ils apporteront chance!*" — So, they will bring luck.

* * *

As on every Sunday morning, the alleys of Polignano
are sleepy, but today perhaps even more than the norm
because it is New Year's Eve, the first day of a new year
in a winter that here seems to be late spring. As I walk,
I arrive at the balcony overlooking the sea. Only a few
hours have passed since the new beginning. Flashes
of sunlight lap against the calm sea: I imagine the
reflections of the coloured lights of the hateful fireworks that will rain on us tonight because there was
no ordinance from the mayor that would hold, or news
of dead and injured to spoil the boor affectation of
those who had persisted in producing or buying them.
Punctual as every year, at the stroke of the first second after midnight the vain fires had let themselves
explode: a moment before, only sterile containers of
variously assembled stars of gunpowder and other
chemical devices; a moment later flown to the skies
of the world to light up the darkness, to rain in the
sea or to reflect on the whiteness of the snow-capped
mountains or on the perspectives of skyscrapers and
old shacks around the world. I've never loved them, the
fireworks. On the contrary. I hated them since I was a
child. Maybe because they have accompanied me every
year since my very first moments of earthly life? Those
same moments, already regrettable per se, which mark
the painful passage from the liquid amniotic world to
the congealed earthly world? Moments of life which
should not force life itself but which unfortunately do
it habitually; I remember them distinctly; I had also

described them several times and as many times I had
been laughed at. "It's impossible to remember certain
things," everyone had always told me. Until Nicola arrived. And with him the birthdays celebrated together
in bed, waiting for midnight to congratulate ourselves,
imagining the colours of the fires in the transparen-
cies of the balloons, with the Armagnac to decant. It
amber red, stubborn as my hair. Because when you
are born with Armagnac-colored hair, no matter how
hard you want to change it with a coat of dye, even
if wisely dosed, you will always remain red, outwardly
and temperamentally. The passion for Armagnac is one
of Nicola's legacies: "Because you are to be sipped like
it, which is a distillate of meditation. It is red like you
and like you it should be sipped with a lot of patience,
like the one that *les maitres de chai* have when they taste
it, in order to be able to classify it," he always said,
more aware than me that I would then study the subject thoroughly.

Nicola always played on this. Even in death. I was
his fertile soil: he planted the seed of curiosity and I
made an entire forest sprout. Only an entire forest can
give you a myriad of green and brown shades; an entire forest can unfold a thousand scents of flowers and
fruits and leaves and grass; only an entire forest can
give you flashes of azure or midnight blue above the
foliage and then treacherously hit you with its blades
of sunny light that slice through the tree branches.

No one else, after him, had ever been able to
replicate his memory: his essence had sublimated everything that had passed through him. A couple of

days after we returned to Polignano, I received a letter from him. I recognized the handwriting immediately: the heart bounced until I withdrew to read it, in the hollow of my window overlooking the sea, still dusty with rubble and plaster. I clumsily opened the envelope, dated and sent on the very day of his death in a surge of awareness before the end, in a last outburst of eternal love towards me. I was in a hurry to make the missive mine as unexpected as it was desired because I had cried about it before even reading it. After that, I dried the tears.

> *My love, infinitely great. If you're reading this it's because I'm gone. I am no longer next to you but I am there and I will be there anyway. What do you have in front of you right now? If I know you well, you will be in front of your sea: well, I'll be in it. I will be that mischievous fish that jumps out of the surface of the water, to capture your attention; I will be that cloud, yes, the one there, up there, sweet as cotton candy of those country fairs that you have always avoided, but of which I have always told you; I will be that bird, yes the very one you now see hovering high, higher than the sky. I will be in everything you look or imagine or dream because you will never need to have me physically next to you again. You never needed it, actually, even though I, selfishly, have always made you believe otherwise. You were my necessity of life, not I yours.*
>
> *Remember the twelve-room theory? Of that Tibetan manuscript, written in the Senzar*

language, that I searched like hell to find but never succeeded? Well, you were my twelfth room, that of the awareness of my everything, the one that closed a cycle of life only to open another though far from the worries and terrestrial affections. Remember when I told you that when a door is closed, a bigger door always opens? You never really understood the meaning of that statement, you took it as pure gold just because it came out of my mouth! You looked at me as if you were peering into my soul, you read into my mind as no one had ever been able to do, you touched my face with your hands in a gesture of ancient memory that undressed me while leaving me dressed. You have been the very essence of what I have called life, and what I have destined for you will find a way to reach you. There is no refuge or salvation from love. In my thoughts, in my pocket or in my soul, it doesn't matter exactly where, I know that I will still be inside you, my great love.

Because everything comes back, because it all makes sense, if you remember it. And memory is reckless: it has no knowledge or rationality, it confuses you, it appears and reappears as it pleases. It grabs you and attacks you when you least expect it. Villainous, it lets itself be breathed with the smells of home, those stale air whiffs that smell of old fried and refried oil, eggplant and onion, mothballs and lavender. It fills your nostrils with the rancid stink from the sea and pee from cats in the corners of buildings because if it doesn't rain badly, it stays stuck there. It lets itself be heard with memories of the sound of bells on Sunday morning, after mass, walking aimlessly in search of coolness, in summer, in the vain aim for shelter from the north-west wind, the mistral, in winter. It makes itself live with the waves beyond the breakwaters and the foam swollen with bubbles and the gusts of air mixed with salt which, despite its transparency, when it mixes its fumes with salt, becomes coloured.

Memories remain in your heart with their colours. Like those of the balconies corroded by the rust of the sea, with their multi-hued redness, which you have to look after every year, unlike the flowers that live on those same balconies with eternal life, accustomed to climatic extremities and the hurried neglect of their hosts. Railings can wear away like rust butter; flowers can't. They give the eyes their due, do justice to the run-down dwellings and, even if left to themselves, come back with new colours and chromatics. They intertwine their experience with other plants, born from the seed brought by a lost bird that in its wandering has decided to stop right there: maybe it has already been there and has returned voluntarily; or else it found itself there and remained there, or it was born there. Then the migratory flows or chance took it away from there. But the memory remains because memory leaves no way out. And it, the bird, even if it has migrated a thousand and a thousand kilometers away, returns there. Where it all originated.

I too had tried to leave and forget, exhausted by events, forced by the life that can let anything happen. But in a perpetual becoming, ungovernable even if programmed to the darkest turns, I had returned there. Where it all started and ended and now it was starting again.

* * *

There is an ancient theory that says that life is made up of twelve rooms. These rooms are those in which we will leave something of ourselves, for future memory, but which we will remember only at the completion of the twelfth: since we are born without the gift of sight, we will walk blindly through the rooms until we reach the twelfth, the room in which we will finally be able to consciously review the eleven lived rooms, to start again from the first room, in an infinite but finally revealed cycle.

Etymologically, the word "*stanza*", Italian for room, derives from the Latin *stantia*, place of residence, in which to stay. The meaning of the word is undoubtedly the least interesting: usually, by room we mean each of the internal divisions of a building, delimited by walls, to which the specific name of the specific space is preferred; we will then have the living room, the kitchen, the bathroom and so on. As you can see, the room is given a particular meaning, which hinges on the image of something that takes up a portion of space, sister of that *stanza* which is the verse of a poem, especially a song or a ballad. In both cases it is a measure, a limitation.

The word "stanza", moreover, means "to stop", but also "to assert oneself". It is an important word, in short, and yet we never think about its real value. We just say it. We give it names, numbers or meanings, sometimes poetic rather than practical: the playroom, the music room, the dream room. The light room or the blind room. The hall, the living room, the bathroom, the kitchen. Rooms are infinite, but we never think about them: they are so common in our life that sometimes we relegate them to being vain, calling them "vani", vain in Italian, or we enslave them, calling them "*camere*"—chambers. And so it happens that we call the rooms where you learn "*aule*", because they are full of air, free because they are full of life, while we call "*celle*"—cells—those rooms where people are locked up, as if they no longer existed, as if they were not visible. There are character rooms: the rooms of joy or pain, the rooms of memory, the abandoned rooms; rooms that are scary, such as those of power, also called "button rooms" or rooms in which to take refuge and still others in which to confine oneself, which are basically close relatives. In short, rooms are truly endless.

Each room has its own sound, its own smell, its own touch and light that affects us and conditions our memory. For each of them, we will open doors that will lead us into another room or out. Because the rooms run into each other. In rooms you enter and from rooms you leave. Rooms may be empty or full and it's us who decide on it, as if we nourish them, or dress them and undress them. Because rooms change, second by second. They change according to the light, at different times of the day or night. They change according to the people who pass through them and who live them:

they absorb our energy and change with the one we leave behind. There are imaginary rooms, created out of necessity, where time does not exist because it remains outside; there are rooms in which we have no body or soul and rooms that are so dark that they remain inside us even when we leave them because they condition our movements, our body, our thoughts.

Yet even dark rooms are important: they make us reflect, they make us think back to the rooms we travelled through before, to the important ones and those always present, to the pleasant and light ones that await us every time we return. The dark rooms take us back to the rooms behind the work of men, which condition their choices or inspire them in spite of themselves. Many of man's creations take place in a room. Life itself is not a time but a space, and space is infinite.

The *twelfth room* is the last of the cycle, but it is never the end of the cycle itself: it is the one from which we start again, from which we are reborn, and we grow up. The twelfth room is that of self-awareness, which together with the acceptance of the "different" way of feeling and seeing things allows us to start all over again.

Acknowledgement

THIS NOVEL IS SET IN A HISTORICAL PERIOD between 1960 and the present day, in Polignano a Mare (BA), my personal "twelfth room". I take this opportunity and space to thank two special women, Polignanesi DOC, who helped me to look at Polignano with their eyes and to speak like them, as if, after all, I really lived there: Assunta Maringelli, a lifelong colleague in Poste Italiane, who patiently guided me through the most hidden alleys, delighting me with glimpses of a Polignano never seen before, and Teresa L'Abbate, historical teacher of Polignano and herself living and lived history with its proverbs and those idioms that captured me and that I used "as a side dish", but served at the table as if they were a whole meal. Entrée, main course, fruit and dessert.

Author's note on Asperger's Syndrome (AS)

In *The Twelfth Room*, I TELL THE STORY of Alina, a little girl with Asperger's syndrome (AS) who discovers this "different feeling" of hers only by the time she is twenty years old. The temporal location of Alina's story, in fact, places the protagonist in a situation of further relational difficulty, as in the years between 1970 and 1980, the years of her adolescence, Asperger's syndrome was relatively unknown in Italy.

Asperger's syndrome is a life condition that involves a different functioning of the nervous system; for many people, this "different functioning" represents a serious problem, above all because the first, real relational difficulty is the failure to recognize a communication code that is common with the rest of the world. In these situations, in fact, children with AS will grow up with the conviction of being flawed and will become, if not understood and "accompanied" in the diversity of the real world, adults unable to carry out their own life plan, even if they have the skills.

Asperger's diagnoses are based on the finding of some common characteristics of behaviour: not all characteristics, however, are always present in the same person and, when they exist, they do not always have the same presentation mode. One in sixty-eight people today is affected by the syndrome or other conditions of the autism spectrum (the word "spectrum" denotes the considerable variability and severity of presentation); therefore, it is a much more frequent condition than is believed.

People with the Syndrome are unable to modulate their reactions and relationships; for them, it is all black or white, and their relational palette of colours does not include others, while they are able, in that white or that black, to grasp all the thousand shades that accompany the gradation, showing significantly superior hypersensitivity or hyper-effectivity to the common average. They are very happy or depressed people and they pass from one state to another suddenly: they always have a reason, but they almost never know how to explain it to themselves, let alone to others. This is why they are often pointed out as crazy, for schizophrenics, for bipolar people, suffering extremely because they are aware of the meaning of the words that mistakenly label them: this is why they tend to further isolate themselves from the world around them, dedicating themselves in an almost totalitarian way to the passion of the moment; from this point of view, people affected by the syndrome range at 360 degrees, delving into everything that becomes a topic of interest to them in a maniacal way.

Females with the syndrome are diagnosed less frequently than males, and not because their frequency is lower. The ability of many girls and girls to be chameleon-like and to find adaptation strategies can mask the difficulties, challenges and loneliness they experience.

Since the knowledge of the characteristics of this "way of functioning" is of great importance to allow people who suffer from it to lead a life like everyone else, a great deal of effort is currently being devoted to spreading knowledge on the subject. As always, when we talk about "diversity", knowledge makes fear go away and brings people together in forms of constructive solidarity and mutual satisfaction, for those who are supported and for those who contribute to this support.

There are countless important personalities, great artists and geniuses of science or technology affected by Asperger's syndrome, alienated from their world but idolized afterwards for their discoveries or artistic creations; this context fits perfectly with the skill of these subjects, autistically divorced from reality though with an IQ that is often above average. It is no coincidence that the Syndrome is placed, from a clinical point of view, among the "high functioning autisms" (HFA), which presupposes difficulties in relating to others where others are not aware of this difficulty: from this point of view, it is therefore important that there is awareness of this "different" condition, to ensure that people with Asperger's syndrome are approached in the way that suits them best. Only in this way is it possible to improve the quality of life not only of affected people but also of those who live with them or with whom they work; the positive results of such an approach, precisely because of the "different" relational modality of the Asperger's, are extremely satisfying, both for one and the other.

This is the story of Alina, of her life in black and white, captured and told in all its infinite chromatic facets. I hope to have succeeded in the intent of delighting and together educating my readers, approaching them to my different way of being and seeing, because only a beautiful story, as if it were Charon, can limbically ferry souls and lead them where the great divine plan has established the location.

About the Author

TERESA ANTONACCI was born in 1964 in the province of Bari (Puglia, Italy) where she currently lives and works. She is a company manager and is married with three children and one granddaughter. *La dodicesima stanza* (translated into English as *The Twelfth Room*) is her fifth book, published by Les Flâneurs Edizioni in 2016. Her other publications include: *Lasciami sognare* (2012), *Rinascerò pesce* (2014), *C'è modo e modo* (2015), *La casa della domenica* (2015), *Enrico fatto di vento* (2017), *Una storia imperfetta* (2018), *Quasi* (2020). She has participated in numerous literary awards and in 2020 she was the winner of the XIV edition of the Premio Giovane Holden with her last book *Quasi*.

About the Translator

CONNIE GUZZO-McPARLAND holds a BA in Italian Literature and a Master's degree in Creative Writing from Concordia University. Upon graduation from the Master's program, in 2007, she received the David McKeen Award for creative writing for her thesis-novel, *Girotondo*. In 2005, an excerpt from this novel, *Verso Halifax*, won second prize at the ninth edition of the *Premio Letterario Cosseria* in Cosseria, Italy. Her first novel, *The Girls of Piazza d'Amore* (Linda Leith Publishing, 2013), was shortlisted for the Concordia First Novel Award by the Quebec Writers' Federation. Her second novel, *The Women of Saturn* (Inanna Publications, 2017) was translated into Italian and published in 2021 by Rubbettino Editore as *Le donne di Saturno*. This translated version won second prize at the 2022 *Concorso Letterario Internazionale Citta di Crucoli, Lucrezia Paletta*, and a special jury award from the 2022 *Premio Vitruvio* (Lecce, Italy). A biography of the operatic Quilico family, *An Opera in 3 Acts* was published in English and French in the fall of 2022 by Linda Leith Publishing. *The Twelfth Room* is her first work of translation. She lives in Montreal and, since 2010, has co-directed Guernica Editions.

MIX
Paper
FSC® C100212

Printed in April 2023
by Gauvin Press,
Gatineau, Québec